Storm warning

"How dare you?"

"How dare I what?"

"How dare you frighten me half to death last night with your darn firecrackers. How dare you let me think you were in the midst of all that shooting. How dare you?"

"Fallen among thieves? I'm a lawyer."

"Same thing!"

"Well!" Jack dragged the word out. It almost served to take him around the table, where he snatched up both Katie's hands just as she attempted to club him with one open palm. "So you really care? I thought I'd be a month getting you to that point!"

"What in the world are you babbling about? Of course I care. I mean I would—" *I mean my mouth has gotten me dead into a possum trap, fool!*

EMMA GOLDRICK describes herself as a grandmother first and an author second. She was born and raised in Puerto Rico, where she met her husband, a career military man from Massachusetts. His postings took them all over the world, which often led to mishaps—such as the Christmas they arrived in Germany before their furniture. Emma uses the places she's been as backgrounds for her books, but just in case she runs short of settings, this prolific author and her husband are always making new travel plans.

EMMA GOLDRICK

Loveable Katie Lovewell

Harlequin Books

TORONTO • NEW YORK • LONDON
AMSTERDAM • PARIS • SYDNEY • HAMBURG
STOCKHOLM • ATHENS • TOKYO • MILAN
MADRID • WARSAW • BUDAPEST • AUCKLAND

To my great-niece, little Katie Clark,
whose determination and lovely red hair
will some day knock 'em all dead.

Harlequin Presents first edition January 1993
ISBN 0-373-11520-2

Original hardcover edition published in 1991
by Mills & Boon Limited

LOVEABLE KATIE LOVEWELL

CHAPTER ONE

KATIE LOVEWELL was the girl who fell asleep on the day of her father's funeral and woke up nine months later wondering what had happened to her life. Oh, not asleep as in the fairy tales, waiting for Prince Charming to come and do his thing. Rather she fell into a daze, in which she ate and slept and worked—and did other things— without understanding or feeling the world that swirled around her. But on the day she woke up everything changed.

Kate could not for the life of her remember why she had come to the party, except that she needed the money. The old mansion, set low on the flank of Massanutten Mountain above the South Fork of the Shenandoah River, was full to overflowing with guests, most of whom were strangers to her. Or she to them. Mrs. Fessenden's invitation had at first seemed like a challenge. A chance to pin Peter down among his own kind. And now she was doing her best to avoid him, and everyone else. They were just not her sort of people.

When the crowd finally migrated from the swimming pool out at the back, swirling like muddy water toward the two open bars in the ballroom, she saw it as a chance to think things through again, and slipped around the veranda and down to the now-empty pool area. Her feet were tired. A full morning at the pre-kindergarten had left her worn, flat, like a bottle of Coke left open too long. The two hours in the courthouse hadn't helped, either.

She settled herself gently into one of the lounge chairs, smoothing her navy knee-length skirt around her carefully, fluffing up the double row of ruffles that centered her white blouse. One more mark of distinction. She had come directly from the district court. Everyone else at the party wore jeans or bikinis or ragged shorts. It never ceased to amaze her how much the rich paid to look poor! Her eyes casually monitored the pair of cardinals settling into their spring routine in the ash trees. The smell of magnolias was almost overpowering. Virginia was coming out of its cloak of winter, flourishing. The noise above her, in the house, was muted by the garden that separated them, and the birds spoke valiantly of another summer to come. She closed her eyes, pulled out the pins that locked her long straw-colored hair at her neck, and leaned back to think it through one more time.

"Are you the baby-sitter?" A tiny voice, almost at her elbow. Kate's eyes snapped open. Looking directly into her green eyes was a pair of childish blue ones, and a little girl, hesitant, unsure. An unruly mop of brown hair, a round pleasant face, a very short body—and a smile which came slowly, sweet enough to tear your heart out.

"Baby-sitter? Do you know some child who needs minding?" And a broad smile of sharing welcome. It was hard not to welcome such a little thing. Eight years old, perhaps? There were gaps between her teeth.

"I—my dad said there was a baby-sitter, while he— oh, here he comes now!" It almost seemed as if the little girl snapped to attention, shoulders back, eyes suddenly neutral. Katie stretched around to see. The man thundering down the path looked ominous. Big, powerful—not too tall, but tall enough. Black hair, black eyes, a Roman nose, and a three-piece suit. She smiled, and twisted at the engagement ring on her finger.

"You there—what's your name?" A gentle baritone, not at all in keeping with the eyes.

"Me?"

"Well, I don't mean Nora. So that only leaves you."

"I guess it does, doesn't it? I'm Kate."

"Kate, I want you to watch Nora for a few minutes. It shouldn't take long to find Fessenden and settle my business. Okay?" The frown had disappeared, along with the promise of murder and mayhem. A pleasant smile replaced it, to match the little girl's, with the same result. It had been a long time since she had been assaulted from two directions with charisma. A nice feeling, that. So I'm a baby-sitter, she whispered to herself. Why not? It's the thing I do best!

"I'd be glad to watch—Nora?" The little girl smiled and moved closer to her chair. Her little hand slid along the arm of the chaise until it slipped under Kate's elbow, and there it stuck. The man nodded his head. He looked ten years younger than he had while thundering down the path. Another smile, equally divided between the two of them, and he turned around and rumbled up the path toward the house again.

"Wow!" Katie chuckled.

"Yeah, well, that's what all the women say," the child offered solemnly. And then with great pride. "That's my dad."

"Wow," Kate repeated whimsically. "Does he have a name?"

"Him? I told you. His name is Dad."

"Yes, I see. Very appropriate, too. And what might your name be?"

"My name is Lenora—but nobody calls me that except the principal at the school when she's mad at me. Everyone else calls me Nora."

And how about that! Kate chuckled to herself. All plainspoken, but leaving no doubt that the poor principal had had to deal with "Lenora" on more than one occasion. Such a gentle creature to be hiding a small devil within.

"Well, Nora, my name is Katie, or Kathleen. How about that for a name?"

"Katie? I don't know anybody else by that name."

"No wonder," she returned wryly, feeling the bite of her own problems. "There's not much of it going around these days."

"You're pretty, Katie."

"You must have some sort of problem with your eyes, Nora. I'm too big—much too big."

"My dad likes big girls."

"So that makes me pretty?"

"What else?"

"Okay," Katie laughed. "So I'm pretty. But let's keep it for our secret, shall we? Look at those lovely birds." The child responded with enthusiasm, but quietly. Only a hiss of exhaled breath disturbed the area as the pair of cardinals chirped at each other and the world.

It was the flurry in the grass at the bottom of the hill that alarmed them both. A quail, nesting in the taller uncut grass, was disturbed, and shot into the air, its wings beating a warning to all the wildlife around it. The warning spread through the scattered trees and a flock of sparrows took wing, wheeling away from the country estate in the direction of an adjacent farm.

"What is it?" the little girl asked, squeezing back against the chair and Katie's arm.

"I don't know. Something's coming up the hill." Kate swung to her feet, herded the child behind her, and gradually backed in the direction of the old apple tree a dozen feet away from the pool area. She was doing her best to remain cool and calm, in order not to alarm the child. When she heard the baying she knew.

"Try a little tree climbing, Nora," she said brightly. The child made an objection, which was overlooked as Katie swung her up into the safety of the lower branches "Can you skedaddle up higher?" she asked cheerfully.

"Sure," Nora returned. "Easy." And set about giving a demonstration. Kate turned back to look down the hill. It was just what she had suspected. Some drunken fool had released the gates on the pen that held the two guard dogs, and they were coursing up the hill in wide sweeps, searching.

It was hard to keep her cool. She could still vividly remember the day when she and her little Border Collie, Shep, had come walking through those woods on the other side of the creek. The guard dogs had been loose that day, too, and Shep had given her life so that her mistress could escape. She swept the scene in front of her, with no idea how much like steel her green eyes looked under pressure. And then back to the little girl, who had managed to scramble two branches higher into the foliage of the apple tree.

"That's the way to do it," Katie called up at the child. Her own hands wrapped themselves around the lower branch of the tree, a sturdy limb some six feet from the ground. With the agility that came from practice she swung herself up into the safety of the tree. Even at that the dogs were almost on her as she pulled her heels up. The two of them, unmuzzled as well as loose, lunged upward on their hind legs, snarling a challenge, baying.

"They look terribly mean," Nora called down anxiously. "They can't climb trees?" The "I hope" was not announced, but understood.

"No, they can't climb trees," Kate said. Her heart was in her mouth as she glared down at the two jumping dogs, and they glared back at her. But the child would suffer if frightened, and that *must* not happen. The secret corner of her heart, which treasured children beyond anything, would just not let it happen. Perhaps a scream for help? She discarded the thought at once. Nora would be more frightened by screaming than by actions.

Luckily the scream was not necessary. The baying of the dogs themselves served as the alarm. Up the hill from behind them the burly figure of the gardener and dog keeper came struggling through the grass. Evvie Hamilton. A friend of her father's, and a man of long acquaintance, armed only with the ultrasound whistle and a pair of leashes. He must have blown the whistle, because the two dogs' ears came up, and both heads turned over their shoulders. Katie relaxed, and gave some attention to herself.

Her neat skirt was rucked up around her waist, there was a conspicuous run in her panty hose, one button had snapped off her blouse, and her hair had come down in a golden mass. She checked out the girl, who seemed to have suffered no damage, and started to make emergency repairs to her own person. It was then that she heard the other roar from up the hill, in the direction of the house. The outraged male, she chuckled to herself. Nora's father, bounding down the hillside with a croquet mallet in one hand, roaring defiance at the dogs and at the world.

The animals themselves were totally confused. A moving human with a weapon represented the one challenge they had been trained to attack, but the relentless whistle behind them ordered recall. Slowly, one step at a time, they retreated downhill, their snarling heads turned in the direction of the new attack.

The pressure off, Kate relaxed against her tree trunk and laughed. Her husky, throaty gurgle tickled the child's fancy. She began to giggle. The racing man, ten feet or more from the tree, heard them both, and slowed to a stop. The dogs continued their retreat until finally they backed right into Hamilton's legs and were quickly leashed. "You okay, Mr. Lee?" the keeper called.

"Out of breath," Nora's father returned, waving a hand. "But I suppose I'll live." He was strolling now, over to the bole of the tree, and looking up. "Lovely. Are you two planning to roost up there all day?"

Katie struggled vainly with her skirts, her face blush red. It was extremely difficult to be modest when perched in a tall tree wearing a short skirt. She had blown her entire image, and that for the *second* time in one day!

"If you've finished leering you might help us down," she suggested coldly.

"I was just about to suggest that. Lovely—er—legs." He held out both hands. "Come on, just jump."

"And you're going to catch me?" It was beginning to be enjoyable. She struggled to keep a straight face. She stood at five feet eleven, and when her comfortable one hundred and forty pounds landed on him there would be some sort of splash indeed! From her position above him it was difficult to see just how tall he was, but his head, clustered in short black curls, looked extremely—attractive? And that wasn't a word she had used for a man in the last several days.

"Well, come on," he repeated. She shrugged her shoulders, and swung her feet around off the branch, disarraying her skirt even further. His eyes seemed to widen as a big grin flashed across his face. She used both hands to lift her bottom up off the branch, and slid down on top of him. His hands grabbed at her just under her arms, and managed to slow her progression, but not enough to avoid catastrophe. She heard him mutter "What the hell" under his breath, and they both hit the ground, he on the bottom.

Somehow or other she found herself sitting on his stomach, his arms wound around her, his hands half supporting her breasts. That second shock was almost as bad as the first. She struggled with his fingers unsuccessfully.

"Lady, maybe if you could get off me," he offered in a very mournful voice. But the pressure of his fingers on the underside of her breasts said otherwise. She broke away with a violent wiggle, landed on her knees, and glared at him.

"Hey," he complained as he rose to his knees. "Don't glare at me. I'm the white knight, aren't I?"

"I don't know," she spat at him. "Sexist, and racist too? There's only one kind of white knight around here. They wear sheets and hide their faces. Look at me!"

It was hard not to cry. The only thing that held her back was her mother's oft-repeated admonition, "big girls don't cry!" And when you had grown to be as big a girl as Kate had that rule was added to all the rest of a growing list of taboos that "big girls" don't do. You didn't cry. She didn't. You didn't hit men in the face, not matter how much you would like to. She didn't. But you did stand up and glare at them. That was allowed. She did.

The surprise was mutual. He clambered to his feet at the same time, and there they were, hardly six inches apart. And my eyes are staring at his Adam's apple, she told herself in awe. She tilted her head back to glare up at him, but the glare failed. Along with her father's name she had inherited her mother's Irish wit. "You'd be a lot taller if you didn't have so much of you bent under for feet," she said pertly.

"You're not such a shrimp yourself," he admitted cautiously.

"Hey, don't I get to come down out of the tree?" the child above them asked.

"Your leg is bleeding," he told Kate. Both his hands were resting comfortably in the indentations of her hips, and he was looking her over inch by inch.

"I believe so," she said, sighing, not moving her eyes for a minute from his face. There was some—attraction—there, but what it was she could not define. And so she drank her fill of him.

"Hey, you two!" Nora had scrambled down to the lowest branches of the tree. "I can't jump from here without help." Both heads below her turned slowly upward. The child was grinning at them. They grinned back. It seemed almost as if space had been crossed after a long voyage, and they were reunited as a family.

"If you don't let go of her you can't catch me," the child giggled.

"I—you wouldn't mind waiting just a minute?" His hands were moving restlessly within a circle of inches at Kate's hips. She caught her breath, not knowing what he might do next, nor what she would do in return. Whatever effect it was having on him, she knew deep down in her that the score was morality zero, excitement ten at that moment.

He did what she least expected. He bent over slightly, kissed her forehead gently, then raised his hands in his daughter's direction. The child whooped, threw herself down off the limb, and was caught safely high in his arms. It seemed to be a game they played often. Kate felt the doors close in her face as they shut her out. She had known them only thirty minutes, and she felt bereft.

Kate managed to rearrange her blouse, and then bent over to check her leg. A twig from the branch had ripped through her panty hose and scraped a three-inch long shallow gash in her skin. The bleeding had almost stopped, and the hurting had begun. But that was another thing big girls didn't do—they didn't admit to hurt and pain. So she didn't.

"Daddy, her name is Kathleen, and she saved my life." Nora, flashing her golden-brown curls in the air around her father's face.

"I don't know how she did it," he answered. "She just reached up and put you on that branch?"

"Yup."

"But that thing is six feet above the ground, and you're going on fifty pounds, little bit." He shook his head in disbelief.

"The dogs were running at us," Kate explained as she brushed herself down. "That adds considerable adrenaline to the system."

"Here, let me help." He set his daughter carefully down on the ground, spun Kate around at the shoulders, and began vigorously to brush her clear of leaf and clinging twiglets. It was not the lightest of brushings.

"I—I think you'd better not go any further," she suggested as his hands reached her hips again.

"I—perhaps you're right," he sighed, disappointment plain on his face.

"I can do the lower bits," the child broke in, and began to pick more foliage off the lower segment of Kate's skirt.

"My name is Lee." He offered a hand and watched approvingly as her own hand, by no means small, slid into his.

"Of the famous Virginia Lees?" The smile was back on her face.

"Not hardly," he chuckled. "The family name was Lesloviciz when my grandfather came over. The Immigration inspectors told him the country wasn't big enough for a lot of names like that, so we became Lee."

Her own smile was cut off abruptly. From up on the hill behind them Mrs. Fessenden was calling imperiously, "Kate! We're about to eat, Kathleen!"

"Duty calls." She sighed, struggling to get her own hand back.

"Duty?" he asked. "Come on, now. You can't be one of the servants in this mausoleum!"

"Not exactly," she told him as she managed to break away and took a couple of limping steps up the hill. "I'm not exactly part of the crowd, and not exactly *not* part of the crowd, if you follow me."

"Well, I don't," he snapped. For a moment she hesitated, unwilling to walk away from the warmth, but she needed the money. Mrs. Fessenden called again shrilly. New money, Katie told herself, married into an old name. Mr. Fessenden—he called himself Colonel Fessenden for no apparent reason—had left to his wife the pursuit of society while he did obscure things and made a great deal more money. Kate's leg bothered her. She limped a step or two up the path, to find a strong arm at her elbow.

"Mr. Lee?"

"John, actually. My friends call me Jack."

"I—I do thank you. I need the help."

"And hate like hell to admit it?"

"I suppose. It's a family trait."

"Family? How many? Where?"

"I—nobody," she sighed as she struggled upward. The pain was diminishing by each step, but she was not about to tell him, and lose the warmth of that arm. "There's nobody left but me."

"I don't even know your last name."

"Yes."

"Aren't you about to tell me?"

"I—only if you promise you won't laugh."

"I promise. With a family name like mine, why should I laugh? I'll never laugh at you, Kate."

"But we've only—just met." And why is it that it's so important to say? she asked herself. Where did all this warmth, this comfort come from? I've had a lot of friends, but none of them made me feel like this.

"We've known each other for centuries," he laughed. "I met you when you were Nefertiti. Remember?"

"Oh, Lord, are you one of those reincarnation people?"

"No, but you're getting maudlin about time," he returned . That chuckle hid behind every word of his, and it built up her excitement. "Don't you feel we've known each other for a long time?"

"I—yes," she admitted. "But surely not Nefertiti."

"I just made that up." His hand tightened at her elbow, and the sun seemed to have acquired a rainbow of delight, which was quickly punctured.

"We're waiting, Kathleen," Mrs. Fessenden fussed. Patience was not the woman's finest attribute. Kate stumbled at the doorstep.

"There's no rush," Jack interrupted. "Kate's been injured by those damn dogs of yours. She needs a few minutes to clean up. Look at her leg!"

"But my guests are starting already, and I *always* have her perform while we eat!"

"You're lucky she doesn't sock you with a half-million-dollar lawsuit," he told her grimly. "Where's the nearest bathroom?"

Mrs. Fessenden drew back in alarm. Half a million dollars was a major amount, even to the *nouveau riche*. She recognized the threat, and *lawsuit* was a word right at the top of her vocabulary. "Kathleen? Surely Kate wouldn't sue me because some——"

"Some idiot——" he prompted.

"Because one of my—guests—accidentally let the dogs loose?"

"The bathroom," Jack interrupted again. "I'll consult with my client." Mrs. Fessenden turned a peculiar shade of purple, and waved a weak hand down the hall.

"I'm your client?" Katie was struggling to contain the giggles.

"My daddy's the best lawyer in the Newnited States." Nora had panted up behind them to join in the conversation.

"United," he corrected absentmindedly.

"Yeah. Like I said."

"Sit over there, Miss—you never did tell me."

"Lovewell," she sighed. "And don't you dare laugh."

"It's not the least bit funny," he agreed. "Lovewell." He enunciated it as if he were tasting it. And was happy with the result. "Now, even a place like this must have a first-aid kit." He slammed his way through the three wall cabinets until he found what he wanted. "You'd better let me help you off with those panty hose."

"I——". Alarm bells went off in her head. Thirty minutes was hardly long enough to know anyone before letting them help you off with your panty hose. Especially when you wore them *under* your briefs. No indeed! She slapped his hands away and stepped back.

"I think...I could get them off by myself—if you would kindly step outside," she managed.

That huge grin was back again. "Spoilsport! Nora, you stay here with Kate, and call me if she gets in any trouble, right?"

"Right, Daddy."

She hurried, fumbled, and consequently took longer than one might have expected before she nodded to the little girl, who promptly called her father back in.

"Put your leg up here," he ordered as he slid a small footstool in her direction. "That's a lovely leg, don't you think so, Nora?" And the conversation went on between father and child, ignoring Kate completely, as he gently washed the injured area, pat-dried it, and applied a soothing lotion.

"Now there it is," he finally announced. "You won't need a bandage."

"I thought you were a lawyer, not a doctor?" she asked.

"I am, but I'm also a jack-of-all-trades."

"John," his daughter prompted. "John of whatever you said."

The man stood up, towering over both of them, both eyes fixed on Kathleen's face. She felt the impact of it. "How would you like to have a smart-alecky daughter like that one?" he questioned. "My name is John." He said it lightly, but there was a tremendous weight of importance behind the words. She could feel it, and nervously licked her lips, not quite sure what to say.

"Nora would make somebody a wonderful daughter, ' she finally admitted.

"Well, *my* momma don't think so," the child snapped. A frown covered the little face.

"That's enough, Nora," her father chided, and tried to change the subject. "Now I don't know what it is that you do, but as long as it isn't ballet dancing I guess you're ready for it, Miss Lovewell."

Miss Lovewell. The camaraderie was gone, along with her first name. Withdrawal symptoms? Or something to do with Nora's mother—who was presumably his wife? Kate stood up carefully and tested her leg. It was stiff, but strong enough to support her. "Thank you for your help, Mr. Lee." She offered her right hand, only to find him ignoring it as he grabbed for her left.

"An engagement ring?" A peremptory tone, distant, chilled, as if he were cross-examining some witness or other. She looked down at her hand in surprise. In all the excitement she had forgotten completely about Peter.

"Yes," she said sadly. "But I won't be wearing it for very long. Just as soon as I get through with this job I'm going to find him. And then I'm afraid it will be all over."

"Oh, wow," Nora said softly, stepping aside to watch them both glare at each other. A knock at the door interrupted the tension.

Mrs. Fessenden had sent a maid this time. A scrawny local girl of sixteen, trying to help support her family. "Excuse me." Kate tried to step around him and get to the door.

"Excuse *me*," he offered. "And thank you for saving my daughter. It was very brave of you."

"I wasn't very brave," Kate muttered. "I was scared to death."

"Ah, but big girls don't scare easily," he chuckled as he stepped aside.

"A lot *you* know," she muttered as she sidled out the half-opened door. "Goodbye, Nora. It was nice to meet you."

"And my daddy too?"

Katie looked down at the little pleading face, and, not understanding the question, managed to create a tiny smile. "And your daddy too," she assured, and hurried out toward the ballroom as fast as her legs could carry her.

Buffet tables had been set up all along the east wall of the huge room. Some of the guests were already wandering down the line, filling plates. The others, the younger crowd, were still clustered around the ornate bar at the far end. And I remember when I danced here, Kate told herself fiercely. When I was a member of the set, and never dreamed things could be different. So young, and such a fool! She made her way over into the corner, where a grand piano sat partly hidden from the rest of the room by potted palms and flowers.

She had brought no music with her, but needed none. It was all part of the Fessenden approach. Pile the classics on top of snobbery, and everyone would applaud. As now. Katie massaged her fingers, positioned the stool, and began to play from memory. Something moving, to begin with. Excerpts from Stravinsky's *Firebird*. And then into softer tone-poems. Smetana's *Die Moldau*, Ravel's *Bolero*, Chabrier's *Espana*, the *Sorcerer's Apprentice* by Dukas, and finally Debussy's classic *Afternoon of a Faun*. A neatly packaged thirty minutes, served up much like the chicken in aspic on the table. A spattering of applause broke the final silence, and suddenly Kathleen became aware she had company.

"I had to find a place to leave Nora," he said. "So this is what you do. And very nice, too. But why here?"

"Because I need the money," she snapped, disturbed by being forced out of her music. It was a hiding place to which she had resorted many times since her mother had died, four years before.

"You could be a concert pianist," he nagged idly.

"I could starve to death, too," she returned bitterly. "Why don't you go away?"

"I'm imposing on you?" A stiff and quick response.

"I don't know. I've got something to do."

"I'll help you."

"No." She held up her hand in a stop-sign gesture. "No. It's something I have to do for myself." No, it's something I don't *want* to do, but I must. Nobody can do it for me. How could I convince anyone that this big, strapping girl was petrified by relationships? That even after what had happened today she was uncertain, confused, doubting?

"Then I'll wait."

"Suit yourself," she sighed, unwilling to argue further. "You're a nice man. Don't get yourself involved with me."

"You're some sort of pariah?"

"You can read about it in tomorrow's paper." She dropped the lid over the keys, rested her hands there for just a moment, then took a deep breath and got up. The guests had finished snacking, and were starting to mill around. She had only to listen to find her target. Peter Lester was larger than life, and noisier too. His baritone bellow could be heard above everything. Strange, it had always been so, but this was the first time she had noticed. He was in the corner, next to the bar.

Kate tugged at her blouse and skirt, took the time to check up on her hair again, and then stalked on trembling legs the length of the ballroom. Peter and his friends. All alike. They were members of the hunt set, and dressed the type. They were also a bunch of complete bores, and sounded like it. And I've known *that* for months, she belabored herself. Years, in fact. So why has it suddenly become so apparent—so unavoidable? How did I ever become engaged to Peter? She knew the answer. She was lonely, and, in the beginning, he had been kind. But that was not the sort of answer she wanted, so she pushed it to the back of her mind. The crowd parted. They had been discussing real estate and some new "in" thing they knew about. Something about her facial expression, or her tall, solid figure, perhaps, caused them to move just that slight distance to create a path for her.

Peter's back was to her. He was busy murmuring some secret to his hangers-on. They were all grinning in expectation of the punch line—to her surprise it didn't seem to be a bawdy tale. She tapped him on the shoulder, and he turned round.

"Oh, Katie! I thought you would want to rest after all that wonderful music."

"Don't fool with me, Peter. You never heard a note. I was watching you. We need to talk, you and I."

"You make life sound so grim, my dear. These are all my friends. You can talk here."

"Not here." Peter, somewhat lubricated at three in the afternoon, was beginning to feel the atmosphere that the rest of his friends had already sensed. They faded away, like wavelets running back down the beach.

"Please, Peter," she begged, tugging at his arm.

"Oh, all right," he muttered. He set his half-empty glass down roughly on the bar, and started out up the side of the ballroom, dragging her beside him. His narrow face was set, angry. He used his free hand to brush the long blond hair out of his eyes. Yesterday she had admired that motion; today it frightened her. But big girls don't get frightened. Oh, Mama, if only you knew what you've done to me, she sighed to herself. Payment is required, and the bill falls due every day!

At the end of the ballroom there was a corridor connecting to the main house. Peter went to the second door to the left, and threw it open. "In here," he muttered. "There's not much chance of any of this crowd coming to the library. I'm not sure any of them can read."

Another thing I hadn't noticed, she lectured herself. He's always so cynical. Always casting himself as so superior. What a fool I've been!

"Well?" The door closed behind them, Peter went directly to the little disc in the center of the floor. As with practically every room in the house, a decanter and glasses stood there. He poured himself a half glass of brandy, and swilled it down in three quick gulps.

"Peter——" She hesitated. He was scowling at her as he slumped into the chair. Why, he doesn't even like me! The thought pierced her. I was going to marry him, and he doesn't even like me! It was too late for that.

"Peter—the—the police came to the house at midday. I——" She had his attention. There was a twisted smile at the corner of his mouth as he looked up at her.

"There was no work at the library," she struggled on, "so I came home early—and—the lock on the door was broken. I don't understand. And then the policeman came. A deputy sheriff."

"And?"

"And he said something about my rights, and asked me a lot of questions about—it was marijuana, Peter. How did marijuana get into my house? Only you and I have keys." The last part of the sentence trailed off into a mutter. Peter was laughing at her.

"You, Peter? Is that why you wanted a key? You?"

"Well, what do you know?" he chuckled. "The lady finally caught on. Yes, Kate, me. What a lovely name. I knew you were the one just as soon as I heard your name." He reached out for the brandy decanter again, and splashed his glass full. "So what did you tell them?"

"Me? I—I didn't know anything. What could I tell them? They said—they made me go down to the courthouse, Peter, and yelled at me and—but I didn't know anything, did I?"

"You'd have to be blind not to know something," he laughed. Strange, she told herself, I always thought it was a boisterous laugh, but it's not. It's coarse—unfeeling.

"So what do you want from me?"

"Peter—they said—I—the court, tomorrow. I have to go, they said. They released me without bail because—because of my father. And tomorrow—you have to come with me, Peter, and tell them it's not my fault. You *have* to!"

"I don't think I've got the time," he chuckled, sipping at his glass. "I have this—er—appointment over in Front Royal."

"You mean with the woman you've been keeping over there?"

"Hey, you really do surprise me. How did you know about Evelyn?"

"I've known for months," she sighed. "I—I thought it was something men did before they got married." It was hard not to sound bitter. Terribly bitter, with a pent-up rage, not against Peter, but against the whole male world.

"Well, you wanted to play reluctant spinster. That's a funny gag for a hulking woman over twenty-five. You didn't expect me to be celibate until you got around to putting out, did you?"

"I suspect not." She leaned forward over the desk, saving up emotional strength for the labor that had to follow. "I think you had better have your ring back," she sighed. It was only a tiny diamond, but she had treasured it for all the months of their engagement. "You won't come to court with me?"

"Of course I won't," he snapped. "How stupid do you think I am?"

There was one spark of fire left in her. "No, I understand, Peter. There's only one stupid one among the two of us, isn't there? What was it you really wanted? My house?"

"Bingo," he laughed. "You finally made the connection. A fine house, out of sight, right on the county border, good access roads. Everything just right." He picked up the ring and toyed with it. "Would you believe how sentimental I am? This was my mother's. I'm glad to get it back."

"Then I must be glad for you. Now, if I may have my key?"

"Which one?" he laughed. He reached into his pocket and pulled out a set of three keys, all identical.

"You had it copied!" The last wisp of control fled as Katie banged the top of the desk with her balled fists. "You had it copied!"

"Twenty-five times," he laughed, struggling up from the chair. He staggered, and the chair fell over, masking the noise of the door opening behind them. "Everybody in our group has a copy," he laughed. "You've had your nose to the grindstone so much every day that we've had a regular ball for weeks. Oh, Katie, you're some kind of landlord, let me tell you!"

She stood stiffly up, back straight, head erect, fists clenched at her sides. If only I could hit him, she screamed at herself. But big girls don't do that! So instead she stood rigid, trembling, repressing even the screams that tore at her throat, the tears that trembled on her eyelids.

But the objection didn't seem to apply to *big men*. John Lee appeared behind her, stalking the man behind the desk. One of his big hands snatched Peter up by the scruff of his neck. The other moved in a short, straight line directly to the side of Peter's jaw, made a vicious cracking sound as it hit, and Peter flew backward over the upset chair, bouncing along the floor until he ended up against the bookcases on the far side of the room.

"Creep!" the big, quiet voice commented to her. She opened her eyes. Two arms were extended in her direction. She walked into them, up against the solid frame of Jack Lee. The arms closed around her, and, despite all the dictums of her childhood, the tall slim girl let loose the tears, sobbing, almost childlike, against the soft sweater. "Oh, God, what am I going to do?" she wailed.

"Everything will be all right," he said softly, stroking her hair. "Everything will be all right." And somehow she almost believed it.

CHAPTER TWO

JACK LEE held Kate long enough for the tears to dry. Peter Lester was stirring on the floor, but just barely. Jack walked over and nudged him gently with the toe of his shoe. "Just make sure that neither you or any of your crowd go near this girl again," he said quietly. It was a quiet demand, yet full of threat, and the man on the floor understood. But there was something in Peter's look which seemed to indicate more trouble to come.

Jack came back to Kate and wrapped her up in his arms again. The pair of them watched as her former fiancé sidled to the door, paused as if to say something, then scuttled from the room. "A real creep, Kate. I don't understand why a pretty lady like you would be engaged to such a—to him."

"I don't either," she said tiredly, nestling just the slightest bit against him. "It's been a confusing year. First Papa died, und then I discovered there wasn't any money. And everyone I thought was a friend turned out not to be. So when Peter came along I was so lonely, and he—damn! I don't want to talk about that right now."

"It's all right, Nefertiti," he comforted. "Here now. Buck up your courage. Nora's in the kitchen, being stuffed with brownies if I guess rightly. Let's go."

They went out into the corridor and back to the same bathroom which they had first used. Kate bathed her eyes hastily, doing away with most of the visible signs of her outburst, then started to fix her hair.

"You always seem to be doing that," Jack chuckled, as he trapped both her hands in his. "Leave it down. I like it that way."

"I'll bet you do," she said wryly. "If it were all curly, the way yours is, I'd understand. Well—all right—just for now." And that's the way it has to be, she thought. I'll do him a favor in return for the one he's done me. After all, we probably won't meet again. Strangers just don't stay in Stanfield. I wish I knew...

"John?" He turned around and looked attentive. "Where do you live?"

"In a motel right this minute," he said. "My daughter and I are gypsying it, looking for a place to settle down. We've been around here for three days. It looks to be a nice area. What do you think?"

"I——" His hand was under her arm, urging her toward the kitchen. "I've lived here all my life. It's nice, but—well, it's a farming center, and you know how badly off the farmers are these days. To make money from grain you have to have a lot of acreage. Poultry is doing well. Tobacco is continually under the gun. Congress could remove the subsidies any day. And the peanut crop is—Lord, they've still got half of last year's crop in storage. The only thing that's holding up is apples, you know."

Why am I babbling so? she thought. He's a lawyer. What the devil does he care about apples? She looked up at him, and wished she had really been Nefertiti.

He tucked an arm under her elbow again, and moved her in the direction of the kitchen. Nora was at the big butcher-block table, chewing on freshly made chocolate-chip cookies. "So I made a mistake in brand," he chuckled. "Come on, little bit. We have to take the lady home."

"That's nice," his daughter managed, mouth stuffed with the crisp cookies.

"You don't have to take me home," Katie interjected. "It's way on the other side of Stanfield, and I have my bike out back."

"Don't you listen, Mr. Lee." Mrs. Milligan, the chief cook and bottle washer, had been eavesdropping shamelessly. "It's eight miles and more down the valley. How that girl ever manages I'm darned if I know. Works her fool head off, she does."

"But I can't just leave my bike here," she protested weakly.

"You don't hafta," Nora interrupted. "We got a rack on the car, don't we, Dad?"

"Indeed we do," he laughed. The hand was at her elbow again, moving her off dead center.

"Don't forget your envelope," Mrs. Milligan called after them as they opened the screen door at the back of the house. Kate flashed her a smile of thanks, and took the little white envelope stuck in the rack just inside the door. He looked at her, curiosity running rampant across his strong face.

"Money," she said pertly. "One mustn't mix money with the social life, you know. So I get my filthy lucre at the back door in a plain unmarked envelope. Half an hour of music, fifty dollars. I don't do half as well at the pre-kindergarten." She could not suppress the wistfulness in the last part of that statement. She loved her music. It had been a great deal of her life. But if push came to shove, children would win out over music any day now. But how did you explain that to a stranger— and a man, at that—without giving him some crazy ideas? She shrugged her shoulders, and let him urge her on.

His car turned out to be a Cadillac. What else? It seemed almost to be blasphemy, strapping her twenty-year-old bicycle on to the back bumper. "It looks just a little out of place," she sighed, as he ushered her into the front seat.

"The car?" he queried. "Well, it's last year's model. We can't all be millionaires." He sounded hurt. She hurried to patch over the misunderstanding, only to see that ridiculous twinkle in his eyes.

"I hope you're having fun out of us country cousins," she snapped stiffly. She turned her head away from him to avoid his open stare.

"You're no relative of mine," he returned. He gunned the motor and swung out on to the old country road. They went through Stanfield in a hurry, then turned south to follow the county road behind Dickey Ridge, parallel to Route 340. She stared at the old, familiar terrain, counted crows in flight, studied budding laurel trees high on the mountain—anything to avoid looking at him. Behind them, Nora maintained an unusual silence for a child.

"Here," Kate said after a few minutes. He slowed, and took the turn into her drive. The old house had never looked better. The sun was already low over the mountain, to the west, and the shadows hid the dilapidation.

"Well, I do declare," he said in an imitation drawl. "Massa lives high on the hog. Where are the slave quarters?"

"Don't be impertinent," she snapped. "You sound like a Yankee. And the slave quarters were all behind the house. General Sheridan burned them all down in 1864. He was a Yankee, I recollect."

"Well, don't blame me," he chuckled. "My family was still in Yugoslavia then. Is this still Warren County?"

"Yes," she sighed. "All this. What are you doing?" He was out of the car and around its front before she recognized what was going on. It was the first time a man had held a car door for her in many a day. She stuttered an apology, which he waved aside.

"We had to get your bike off," he said. "Nora, come help Kate get her machine unbuckled." And with that he wandered off toward the house.

"Well, I'll be——"

"You'll be what?" the little girl prompted.

"I—I don't know what I'll be," Kathleen giggled. "Didn't I hear him say he was going to help me with the bike? And then he walked off?"

"Fathers are like that," the child responded very maturely. "I think that's what they call in school having short attention span. You think so?"

"How would I know, love? He's your dad, not mine. What do we do now?"

"Well, you hold the frame while I unbuckle this snap-fitting here." And the bicycle came off the complicated mount without a bit of trouble. By that time Jack had wandered back.

"Smashed your lock," he said. There was a contented sound in his voice, as if a smashed lock was a welcome challenge. "Where's the nearest hardware store?"

Kate was tired. It came over her suddenly, an emotional tiredness which had drained all her batteries. She longed for a place to sit down, and the porch was closest. "Down there." She waved generally southward. "Bentonville." Her legs managed the short distance to the porch, and she thumped herself down on the second step.

He came over and squatted down in front of her, taking her pale face between his hands. "Tired? Too much for you? Do you think you can survive for a few minutes?" And then, without waiting for an answer, he stood up again. "Nora, you stay here with Miss Lovewell while I go get us a new lock for her door."

The child showed that odd maturity again, coming over to sit beside Kate, putting a small arm around her waist, nodding with understanding. The father trotted back to the car, and kicked up a few pebbles as he returned to the road.

"That's a strange man," Katie said as they watched the brake lights on the car sparkle for a second at the corner. She looked down at the girl. "And you're a strange one, too, aren't you, Lenora?"

"Who, me?" The child returned a gamine grin, and whipped a crumbled cookie out of the pocket of her denims. "Want a cookie?"

Kate glanced at the wreck of the cookie and shuddered. "I—I don't think so. I'm not very hungry."

"That's the trouble," the child insisted. "You didn't eat no lunch——"

"Any lunch," Kate corrected.

"Any lunch. And you need some coal in your burner. Well, that's what Dad says."

"And if Dad says, it must be right?"

"Why, of course!"

For whatever reason, Kathleen found herself munching on the cookie, her eyes trained on the hills. The ball that was the sun sat just on the tip of the Massanuttens, flashing red and yellow and russet.

"There's a lot of mountains around here," Nora offered after a few minutes of silence.

"Indeed there are. But not where you come from?"

"We come from Washington. DC that is. As far as I know there ain't no——"

"Aren't any"

"Yeah—there aren't any mountains in Washington. Just statues and senators. Dad says they're both alike—the statues and the senators, I mean. If the senators don't keep moving people begin to think they're statues. I didn't like it there at all. You can breathe better out here."

"Yes, that's true." They both took an exaggerated breath. It *was* nice in the valley. There was the blossom-smell of the laurel high on the mountain, the sweet, heavy scent of unturned earth, and the laughter of the river as it ran in front of the house. Another moment of silence. What better chance? Kate asked herself. A dirty trick, picking on the kid, but how else do I learn? *He* obviously isn't going to give me the time of day unless it suits him! "Does your mother like it around these parts, Nora?"

"Huh!" A disgusted grunt. "How would I know?"

"Well—you must know *something*——"

"Yeah, sure. When I was one years old she ran away. I ain't never seen her since. And don't tell me I can't say ain't, 'cause I can!"

"I—I wasn't going to." And that's a red-faced lie, she thought. It's so darn automatic, after working at the school, to correct everyone's English. What a stupid idea. And now Nora needed soothing.

"You don't seem to have suffered from it," she suggested. "Look what a lovely child you've turned out to be!"

"That's not what they said at the school," the girl announced grimly. "That's why we had to—that's why we moved out of Washington. Daddy says they were all a bunch of—oops. He told me never to use those words at all. Never."

"Wow!" And another silence. "Want to see over my house?"

"It's all your house? Yes, I'd like to see it." The pair of them stood up, joined hands by mutual consent, and walked into the big house. They were on the third floor when the horn sounded outside, heralding Jack Lee's return. Nora clattered down the stairs to meet him, throwing herself at him desperately as if he had been gone on an exploration to Mars.

"And Daddy, would you believe it, they have fourteen bedrooms! Fourteen! Of course lots of them are little, up on the top floor, for the servants, you know, but the rest are somethin', believe me."

"Oh, I believe you, princess," he chuckled. He set down his packages by the front door, stripped off his jacket, and looked around. "An electric outlet?"

"Over here." He plugged in an electric drill, and began at once.

"Had to buy a drill, too," he explained as he kept his head down in the work. "Didn't bring a single tool with me. Fourteen bedrooms, huh? How many baths?"

"I don't remember," Nora laughed. "I was so busy counting beds and things. Some of the rooms don't have nothing in them."

"Fourteen bedrooms, and only four baths," Kate interjected. "Everybody needs to sleep. Not everybody has to take a bath—well, not all at the same time."

He stopped work to look up at her. "Don't be apologetic," he advised. "Four baths is plenty—depending on how many people there are to bathe."

She refused the gambit, and after a minute or two he went back to work. By five o'clock, he had removed the old broken lock, replacing it with a new deadbolt affair, which he carefully explained. "It looks as if the old one was put on years ago," he commented.

"Yes," she said with a perfectly serious face. "Right after General Sheridan burned down the slave quarters." He shook his head slowly, and she was unable to repress the giggles.

"She's funnin' you, Dad," Nora broke in.

"I can see that. Why do you suppose she would do that?"

"Because I think she likes you."

"Do you think so? Shall I ask her?"

"It must be a ball of fun living in a house with you two," Kate commented dourly. "A pair of comedians, no less. I thank you for fixing my door."

"And what do you suppose she means by that, Nora?"

"I think she wants us to check the door from the outside, that's what."

"Well!" He stood up, gathering his tools together. "I can take a hint. I suppose she expects us to sweep up all this sawdust, too?"

"No, she doesn't." Kate barely managed the words. Giggles were getting in the way. "She's more than capable of sweeping up a few bits and pieces. And I really *do* thank you—and not just for fixing my door, either."

"You know what you ought to do, Daddy?"

"No, what?"

"You ought to kiss her."

"You think that would be a good idea? Why don't you tote these things out to the car for me." The child hefted the bag, and started for the door.

"No—I—take your father with you," Kate pleaded.

"Go ahead, Nora."

Kate backed away from him slowly. He followed. The grin he wore seemed to cover his whole face. The curly black hair, disarranged during his work, crowded down over his forehead. The dark, dark eyes positively sparkled. The widespread lips revealed a firm line of teeth that seemed to get bigger and bigger the closer he came, until she could see nothing but the gleam of his eyes, the sparkle of his teeth. His head bent over, hovered, poised, and dived at her lips.

It was like a whisper of a promise. A momentary contact that left a taste of sweetness behind. "Katie?" he murmured. She was too busy to answer. Too busy wrapping her hands around his neck, pulling his head down to repeat that magic touch. He seemed to hold back for a second, and then joined in. The second touch was not that fluttery promise, but a warm moist meeting of two souls. It lasted until Kate ran out of oxygen; their lips parted reluctantly, and for a moment or two he stood there, looking down at her enigmatically.

"Are you sure you don't have something else to tell me?"

"I—no," she stuttered, not even remembering what he might be talking about.

"Then I guess I'd better go," he said. His arms unfolded and released her. She took a half step backward, nervously rearranging her blouse, which didn't require any attention at all.

"I'd guess you'd better," she said softly. "It was— nice meeting you. Perhaps we might run into each other some other day?" Did I make that too much of a pleading? Or is this goodbye? I don't want to say goodbye. Not to you!

"Oh, I'm sure we'll be seeing each other," he returned. He squeezed her waist with both hands, then turned on his heel and made off. She followed him to the door, standing with it open, watching, as he strode down to the car, climbed in, and drove off. From the passenger side a little hand waved at her. She returned the salute, and then watched. Watched for another ten minutes, staring at the empty road, and the settling dust which his tires had kicked up. Just staring.

Fourteen bedrooms, four baths, six family rooms of various sizes, one huge kitchen, and one occupant. The thought hit her in the face as she closed the door behind her, shutting out the world, and locking her into her own private corner. One large house, two hundred and forty acres of land, and not a penny of income, save what she could pick up from odd jobs. As she straggled back to the kitchen it was hard to keep the tears from her eyes.

How the place had bustled when she was young! Life had danced. Her beautiful mother had been the core of local society—until the accident that killed her. And after that her father—her pillar—had turned inward, neglecting everything, until lung cancer ended everything.

"I'm sorry, Miss Lovewell," the family lawyer had said on the day of the funeral. Harry Bledsoe, in his late sixties, a dry stick of a man who had managed to stir a compassion for the young woman in front of him. "By the terms of the will you inherit the house, the land—and just enough money to pay the inheritance tax."

"But Mr. Bledsoe, there was my mother's money——"

"All gone, my dear. It was illegal for your father to touch it, but he *was* your guardian. And he spent it all."

"I—but what can I do?"

"Kate, there's only one answer. You have to sell the place. It's a bad time to sell farm land, but the house might bring something reasonable."

"I—I can't just make a decision like that." The lawyer was surprised to see the tears. He felt just like half the world did. Big girls just *didn't* cry. Spartans, they were supposed to be, able to bear anything.

"There's time," he offered tentatively. "The will must be probated, accounts settled, taxes recomputed. I doubt if it can be done in nine months. You have that much time."

"But then you'd advise me to sell?"

"Yes."

And now there was only a month left. Thirty days of April. She had done her best, but, untrained in the available jobs, she had not succeeded. A part-time librarian, a teacher's aide at the kindergarten, a part-time musician. In a world full of well-trained specialists there was hardly room for the partially trained. And the best she had come up with was to sell out, take what money resulted, and go back to Richmond for training. In something. What a life goal that would be. Training, in *something*!

It was a question she took to bed with her every night. A problem she awoke to face, still unsolved, every morning. As she puttered through the mechanics of a simple supper it bothered her as she worked.

She was on the stairs at nine o'clock, on her way up for a bath, when three cars drove up into the drive, their headlights bouncing off the old house, and their horns blaring away. Somebody tried the front door, then pounded on it. I should have got a dog, she told herself grimly. Two dogs. The pounding continued. There was an old shotgun in her father's den. Solidly rusted, with no cartridges to fit, but it *looked* impressive. She fetched it, and made her way to the door.

The pounding continued. She leaned against the inside of the door, resting her head on the solid oak panel, and prayed that they would go away. Instead the noise level grew; somebody was singing "Shenandoah" very much off-key. Others were trying to help. The door rattled as a weight was thrown against it from the outside. It was useless just to stand, hoping. She fastened the safety-chain, turned the deadbolt key, and opened it.

Peter Lester was on the doorstep. "Well, it's about time," he announced. "My key won't fit. Open up, Katie. We've come to have a party."

"You're drunk," she answered disgustedly.

"Not yet. But I will be. Open up." He turned around and yelled to the crowd in the cars. "Come on up. We'll have a big time. I've got an awful lot of girl up here!"

The roar of laughter snapped Katie out of her stupor. There were eight of them. Enough to make big problems. Enough to do a great deal of damage. She flicked on the porch lights, then thrust the muzzle of the shotgun through the partially opened door.

"Peter, can you see what this is?"

"Why, I do believe it's a shotgun," he crowed. "Is it real?"

"Try touching it," she suggested.

He stretched out a finger and laid it on the cold gun-metal muzzle. "Why, I do believe it is. So what, Kate? You couldn't hurt a flea."

"If you want to think so," she said softly. "Remember today, Peter? You broke our engagement, and got me arrested. Remember that? And now you've come up to my house after dark and threatened me."

"Me? I haven't threatened you." The bluster had gone out of him as the hole in the muzzle of the gun tracked the middle of his stomach.

"Oh, yes, you did, Peter," she continued, trying to fill her words with steel. "You threatened me. That's what I'll tell the sheriff, you know."

"But I'll tell him differently," the man said uneasily.

"There. You did it again," she chuckled. "You threatened me again. And how could you tell the sheriff anything, Peter, after I've blown your stomach away?" She moved one hand to the breach of the gun and thumbed at the hammers. One of them moved with a deadly click. It was enough. The man she had planned to marry backed slowly and quietly down the stairs, climbed back into his car, and slammed the door.

Peter leaned his head out of the car window. "But I'll be back," he yelled. "I'll be back." The rest of his crew had become strangely silent. They followed as he drove away.

Totally drained now, Kate slammed the door shut, affixed the deadbolt lock, stood the shotgun up in the corner by the door, and for the first time in her life toured the entire house, making sure all the doors and windows were closed and locked.

There was barely enough hot water for her bath. The water heater and the furnace itself needed replacement. She sank into the tub, immersed herself thoroughly in the last of her bubble bath, and did her best to relax. It was hard to do. "I'll be back," Peter had yelled. And he surely would. She knew enough about him to realize he had a mean streak ten miles long and remembered a grudge better than an elephant could.

"So how come you planned to marry him, dummy?" she asked the empty room. And had no answer. Because

I've been in a daze since Dad died? Because I'm a misfit in this crazy world. The world is made for little people. If David and Goliath were battling right in front of me now, I'd cheer for the giant! At least *that* brought a little grin to her face. It gave her the courage to look into the mirror and not reject what she saw.

"You could have lovely hair if you brushed it," she told herself very firmly, and proceeded to do just that. In the end it looked less like straw and more like thin-spun gold, falling down over her breasts, reminding her. She slipped her flannel nightgown over her head reluctantly, wanting for one more minute to stand foolishly nude before the mirror, and dream.

The bed was warm. When the furnace had packed up she'd had enough money for an electric blanket. It served well. She dived into its warmth, coiled up on her side, and daydreamed. Lenora Lee. What a lovely child. I could go for a kid like that. Who are you kidding, Kate Lovewell? That's not the Lee that draws your attention! Jack Lee. What a lovely face. I wonder how many thousand women he's kissed like that? I wouldn't care how long the line was if I were the last! I wonder how it would be if he were here right now, right here?

She had read a great many books about the subject, but had no practical experience. So it was no wonder that as she fell asleep she was blushing.

CHAPTER THREE

THE next day Kathleen woke up to an early morning haze. A cloud had settled on the valley. Only the tops of the mountains projected high into the sunshine. It would soon burn off. Kate was not one of those who woke up laggardly. With her it was instant awareness and eagerness to be about the day. But for this one morning it was a pleasure to lay abed.

She stretched to her limit, toes touching the old ornate footboard, hands flat against the headboard. There was a sensuous feeling to it all—a feeling of renewal. All her separate muscles made report as she squirmed in the warm bed, and their message was *happiness*. It was as if, suddenly, the past year had been completely excised from her memory, making her once again the cheerful, sensible girl she had always been.

But the clock haunted her. It was an old pendulum timepiece whose face registered to within the minute, but whose chimes were always ringing two hours ahead. And at the moment it was sounding a false "nine o'clock." She slid out from under the blankets, shivered in the slight chill of early spring, and made a dash for the bathroom.

You have a part to play today, she told her mirror image. You have to convince Judge Pettibone that you're still the solemn, sincere Katie who he has known for all your years.

The weatherman had predicted a warm day, despite the morning chill. So a neat shirt dress, dark brown, with low shoes—the judge was a small man himself. A little flash of color at the throat—the pale yellow scarf her mother had chosen for her. And hair, brushed for its full hundred strokes, then braided—and put up? No. Left hanging behind her, halfway down her back. No makeup. The judge was seventy years old. Well, perhaps a little light lip gloss. A touch of perfume, a jacket in case the weather predictors were wrong, and down for a cup of coffee and two pieces of toast.

She had been summoned to the court for ten o'clock, the first case on the docket. It took almost that long to prepare herself and then pedal the old bicycle the distance into town.

Stanfield was one of the really old towns in the valley, with narrow streets, houses set back from the pavements, trees lining the main streets—both of them. Industry was seeping into the valley. Up north at Winchester, over at Harper Ferry. Even a few miles away, at Front Royal. But not yet to Stanfield. A brick court house, built before the war between the states, was set on the top of a small hill, with full lawns surrounding it, a few shaded trees, and a monument. A commemoration to T.J. Jackson and his foot cavalry who had camped on that lawn one night in 1862. General "Stonewall" Jackson, that was.

A bleary-eyed bailiff met her at the door of the district courtroom, and ushered her to a front seat, conspicuously alone. Three or four other people huddled in corners, waiting for cases to be called.

She settled into her seat, and felt the gloom of the old building descend on to her shoulders. The bench was as old as the building. Lord knew how many women had sat right here and felt the same, she thought. Keep your spirits up. Smile! It was a hard order to fill.

The door at the back of the chamber opened, and Judge Pettibone, complete in black robes, came in. The bailiff chanted an unrecognizable litany, culminating in "All Rise." The rustle throughout the room caught her by surprise. She turned around quickly. While she was dreaming, the place had filled. A flashbulb went off in her face. She blinked her eyes, and turned to the front again. The judge sat down in his easy chair, settled himself, and banged the gavel. Everyone sat down. Katie followed suit.

Judge Pettibone fumbled through a handful of papers his clerk had set before him, and cleared his throat. "In the case of the Commonwealth of Virginia versus Katie Rosalie Lovewell, an arraignment. Mr. Prosecutor?"

"The state is ready, your honor."

"And Little Rosie—er—Miss Lovewell?" She looked up, startled. He had always called her Little Rosie, ever since the day she had topped him, on her tenth birthday. "You have no lawyer, Kate?"

"I—no, your honor. I—I don't have the money for a lawyer."

The judge sighed. "You understand, this is not a trial. This is an opportunity for the state to demonstrate sufficient evidence to make a trial necessary. But it is an important step in law. You need a lawyer. Shall I appoint a public defender?"

"I—I really don't——"

"She has an attorney." A pleasant baritone voice from the back of the court. She didn't need to turn around. It was Jack Lee. She hunched herself down into her jacket collar. If there was any single thing she *did not* want this man to know, this was it. And here he was. My lawyer? God. I not only need a lawyer, I need a keeper!

"Er—Mr. Lee, is it?" Judge Pettibone was having trouble with his bifocals. He took them off and wiped them with a handkerchief. "We don't often have such well-known attorneys in our area. You are licenced to practice in Virginia, Mr. Lee?"

"I am." He ambled down the aisle, briefcase in hand, and squeezed on to the bench next to Katie.

"Miss Lovewell, is Mr. Lee acceptable to you in this case?"

I ought to be happy, she told herself, as she huddled miserably in the seat. I ought to—cry. Why him, Lord? She made a stab at her eyes. He leaned over. "You're supposed to smile and say yes, and look very, very confident," he whispered.

"I—it's very hard to do," she managed to mumble. The judge was waiting patiently. "Yes," she announced.

"My client and I need a moment or two to confer, your honor."

"Of course. Take what time you need." The gavel thumped, and the judge went back to his paper shuffling. Across the room the local prosecutor, Tom Gerney, glared at the defense, and then shrugged his shoulders. Jack leaned closer to Katie, dropping one arm on the bench behind her.

"Nora tells me that thirteen of your fourteen bedrooms are dusty," he whispered.

"Well, I can't be everywhere at once," she returned defensively, startled by the turn of conversation.

"So you could have one of the servants dust?"

"I don't have any servants," she whispered stormily. "Just me."

"You mean you spent the night alone in that monster of a house? Suppose somebody came?"

"Somebody did," she snapped loudly, and then blushed as everyone in the court turned in her direction. She dropped back down to a whisper. "How am I going to get out of this horrible situation?"

"Don't worry about a thing," he chuckled, patting his briefcase.

"Yes, that's what John Brown's lawyer told him just before they took him away," she replied sharply. "What have you got in that valise, papers?"

"Who was it?"

"Who was what?"

"Who was it that came in the dead of night? Lester?"

"I—yes. I sent him away."

"Just like that?"

"No—not just like that. It took a little doing. I—I threatened him."

"The talk around town is that Katie Lovewell is a big, softhearted girl who wouldn't hurt a fly."

"You shouldn't listen to gossip. I've hurt a lot of flies in my day. But I—I'm afraid he might come back again." That in a tiny whisper that faded away into silence almost before it was completed.

"I don't think so. He can't walk around much with a broken leg."

"You—you broke his leg?"

"Not yet. I'm a great psychic, though, and I see a terrible accident about to happen to Peter Lester."

"I—I——"

"You don't approve of violence?"

"I thought all lawyers obey the law! What's in the valise?"

"All lawyers do," he whispered sternly. "Me, I'm a Yugoslavian shyster."

"Oh, my." And then, for want of something else to say, she repeated her question. "What's in the valise?"

"Four sandwiches," he whispered, moving closer to her ear. "Nora made them this morning. You can have your choice of bacon and egg, or egg and bacon."

"I—I don't understand!" But she did. The devil was gleaming at her out of those dark eyes of his, and the corner of his mouth was flicking back and forth the tiniest bit.

"That's just what I need," he chuckled softly. "A confused client. Now, all you have to do is keep your mouth shut—unless I stab you in the rib like this." He demonstrated by tickling her just under her lowest rib. She jumped, wondering how he knew her sensitivity at just that particular spot.

"And when I do that," he said very urbanely, "you look the judge straight in the eye and say 'yes, sir.' Got it?"

Katie was beginning to regain her composure, her light-heartedness. She could not see how this mess would be straightened out, but this certainly was the man to do it. Still, he needed taking down a peg. "Is it all right if I say 'yes, sir, Uncle Victor'?" she asked primly.

"Oh, my," he laughed. "So that's how it is!" The gavel thudded on the judge's desk.

"Your honor." He stood up. She looked up at him, wondering why it was that her world seemed so much more secure. "We are prepared." The old judge peered at them both, then took off his glasses again and wiped them nervously.

"You agree, Katie?"

"Yes, sir," she whispered, and blushed again as Jack dropped into the seat beside her and tickled her. "Yes, sir," she repeated, as loudly and firmly as she could.

The judge smiled at her, rapped the gavel, and sat back. "Mr. Prosecutor?"

Tom Gerney, the prosecutor, got up from his chair like a whale coming to the surface for oxygen. "The state has one witness, your honor, and some material evidence, which indicates that the defendant is guilty of possession for sale of a Class Three substance—namely, marijuana. I call Deputy Paine, of the county sheriff's office."

"I know him," Katie whispered to her attorney as the young man was sworn in. "He's a terrible dancer. Awful."

"That won't have much impression on his police work," he advised. "Tell me something interesting."

"Well, he likes to use his muscles. You know, the strong-arm type. He sees himself as another John Wayne. I'll bet he broke my door lock."

"Now that's interesting," her counsel chuckled.

"And so he was speeding, and I chased him," the deputy was saying. "And he pulled up in front of this house and ran in and locked the door behind him."

"This house was that of the defendant?"

"Well, sure. Everybody knows where the Lovewells live."

"So go on, please."

"So he wouldn't come out. I went around the house trying all the windows, and I figured I had to go in through the front door, you see. So I did. I kicked the door open, and there he was. Jeff Filmore. A cousin of the Lester family, your honor."

"I know," the judge sighed. The point had just broken on his doodling pencil. "Please go on."

"Well, anyways, there he was, and right on the table in the hall was this little plastic bag of leaf. So I gave him a citation for speeding, and a lecture, and I brought this here bag back to the station." The young man smiled, as if the recitation had been harder than the arrest.

"And chemical analysis of the contents of the bag, your honor, indicates it to be marijuana. Shall we produce the technician, your honor?"

"Mr. Lee?"

"No, your honor. The defense wants to save the county as much money as it can. We'll stipulate that the bag is filled with marijuana. Or anything else the prosecution wants to call it." The judge's gavel thumped a time or two. "None of that," the old man cautioned.

"Then that's our case," Mr. Gerney concluded. "The house belongs to the defendant. The marijuana was found in the house. There is enough evidence to bring the matter to trial." He moved back toward his desk in the well of the court. The young deputy started to get up, but stopped as Jack Lee came over to the stand.

"You know, your honor," he said conversationally, "I do believe we might save the county even more if I might ask a question or two?"

"Most unusual," the prosecutor mumbled.

"But it has a nice ring to it," Judge Pettibone conceded. "Go ahead, Mr. Lee."

"Well, now, Deputy——?"

"Paine," the young man offered nervously. There was something authoritative about this big wheel from the nation's capital.

"Yes—Deputy Paine. You were chasing this young man—Mr. Filmore, I believe—on a speeding charge?"

"Yes. Eighty miles an hour, he was doing, right up Main Street."

"And if you caught him you were going to arrest him?"

"Oh, no. A traffic citation, and a good lecture. Unless he was drunk. Which he wasn't. Scared, but not drunk."

"So, he had committed a misdemeanor. Not a felony. Just a misdemeanor; if it *was* a crime, it was a very tiny one. Now, tell me again about breaking down the door."

The young policeman fingered his too-tight collar, and thought for a moment. And then his face lit up. "Well, sir," he said. "I was in, like, hot pursuit. That's what we call it in——"

"I know." Jack smiled back at him. "Go ahead."

"Well, as I said, I was in hot pursuit of a criminal, and he hid behind a locked door, so I broke in."

"And of course you had a search warrant in your pocket?"

"Now why would I carry somethin' like that around?"

"You mean that you really had no suspicions about the contents of the house *before* you broke down the door?"

"Why, of course not. I told you. It's the Lovewell house. I didn't have any suspicions."

"Of course not. You were in hot pursuit."

"Well, yes. We can break in any place where there's a criminal we're chasing."

"And this Filmore fellow. He had a key, did he?"

The deputy stammered. "To tell the truth he had two keys. I brung them to court if you want to——"

"Ah, yes. Of course. I don't think we need to see the keys in this case, Deputy. Now, you broke in—smashed the door lock, to be honest about it? Unfortunately there wasn't any criminal inside the house, was there, Deputy Paine? All you intended was to give a traffic ticket.

That's not exactly a criminal offense in itself. So you didn't *see* a felony being committed. All you saw was a misdemeanor. Too bad." The young deputy sagged back in the witness chair, his mouth hanging open.

Lee turned to the judge, who was busy inspecting his fingernails. "Your honor will recognize, of course, that in the case we have before us the officer had no legal right to break down the door, and therefore whatever he may have found inside cannot be considered in evidence against my client. I move for dismissal of the charges."

"Granted." The gavel banged before Lee had finished the sentence. "Case dismissed. Go home, Rosalie."

"But your honor——" Gerney was struggling up out of his chair again, but the judge had gone. Katie stood up, startled, confused. Her lawyer had gone over to the prosecutor's desk.

"Strange, isn't it?" he said loudly enough for the few reporters to hear. "Filmore is in the house with the drug, but it's my client, who wasn't even home at the time, who gets arrested. Whatever happened to Filmore?"

"He offered to turn state's evidence, for immunity under *this* charge," Gerney muttered.

"Stupid," Lee returned gruffly. "Even a second-year law student could see the hole in it. I wouldn't want to see my client suffer from any further harassment. Not any." He was tapping the table in front of the prosecutor's nose with one heavy finger, to emphasize the words.

"Now then, Katie, about this other matter." He came smiling back across the courtroom, and took her elbow.

"Y—you mean I'm free? That's it?" she stuttered. "I don't have to—to go to jail?"

"You don't get to pass GO either," he chuckled. "Or collect two hundred dollars. Stupid case."

"But—but I'm not found guilty? Or not guilty either?"

"I'm afraid that's the way the cookie crumbles." She could read the sympathy in his eyes, but was determined not to be a public watering pot. In private, maybe—but not in public. She tilted her head back, squared her shoulders, and marched out of the courtroom beside him as if she hadn't a care in the world.

"Miss Lovewell," one of the two reporters interrupted, just as they reached the door.

"My client has nothing to say." Lee did not exactly push the man aside, but just flowed over the space where he had been standing. "My client and I are considering suing a few people in this town." And by that time they were on the pavement, and there was the Cadillac, standing in a "No Standing" zone.

"No parking ticket?" she ventured as he closed his door behind him.

"Not a chance," he laughed. "God smiles on the daring. Or something like that. Now, I want you to know how valuable those sandwiches are. Did you ever try to keep house in a motel? Nora's not too happy about it, and we have to stay in this area for a little more time. I just don't know what we'll do."

She looked at him thoughtfully. "You must have been a ham actor at one time or another," she prodded. "That's a terrible act you're putting on. This is where you turn on the weepies, and pray for a roof to put over your only child's head—she is your only child, isn't she?"

"Yes. Do go on."

"And how terrible it is to be cast out in the snow without kith or kin or——"

"Well, it's cloudy over the mountain. That *might* be snow."

"Hah! In April we don't have snow in Virginia. It's in the State Constitution."

"My mistake. You have lovely hands for such a big girl."

"If you say that again I'll *hit* you."

"Say what?"

"Big girl," she simpered. "I'm damn sick and tired of being a *big girl*!"

"It's all relative," he laughed, and drew her over beside him. "There. You don't look too big. Not to me. Try the head on the shoulder bit." It was a nice offer. She gave it a try. It was a very good fit, her head on his shoulder. Very comfortable. She closed her eyes for a moment, and when she woke up they were parked in front of the motel, his shoulder was gone, and he and Nora were carrying suitcases out of the double room.

"Oh, that's so nice of you," Nora yelled. "I couldn't of stood that motel another night. Not one more night. Thank you, Katie!" The "thank you" was accompanied by a very large, wet kiss from the back seat. "You're wonderful!"

"Yes, I am, aren't I?" Katie returned, trying to fight her way out of the morass. "What am I wonderful for?"

"For inviting us to stay in some of your fourteen bedrooms," the child said gleefully. "Can I have one at the top?"

"Now we mustn't hurry Miss Lovewell," her father interrupted. "She has a great deal on her mind, and I'm sure she's forgotten a thing or two. Run back and check the room, Nora. We wouldn't want to leave anything behind."

Katie watched the little girl skip as she headed back to the room, and then turned to examine the father. He stood her inquisitorial inspection with pure innocence written all over his face. "I did invite you, did I?" she asked.

"I think Nora had the right idea." He was into the front seat beside her before she could formulate her thoughts. Both arms came around her shoulders, tugging her in his general direction. She put up her hands to maintain her private space.

"Just a darn minute!" she protested. "I need to know what's going on here, counselor. Just when was it that I invited you and your daughter to move in with me?"

"Why, just before you fell asleep," he said meekly. "I was telling you that——"

"Yes, I remember that part. You were telling me a sad, sad story about Nora being penned up in a motel room. That I remember."

"Well, she *thinks* you invited her, and I'd hate to see her disappointed, wouldn't you?"

"Darn you. It's all a put-on, isn't it? Why me?"

"Because," he sighed, and added a little tug to the pressure of his arms. Her resistance collapsed immediately. In fact, she helped a little by sliding along the seat until they were thigh to thigh. And then, in one little helpless shrug, she collapsed across his lap, pinned between his chest and the steering wheel, while he nibbled on her ear deliciously.

"That's why," he said softly a few minutes later. "I wish you wouldn't wear earrings. They take all the fun out of ear nibbling."

"Do they really?" she returned vaguely. It had been such a pleasant minute. One hand was already up unfastening her little gold studs when a thought hit her.

"That child is taking a long time just to check a couple of rooms."

"You sound very suspicious."

"Well, I can't help it. That's the sort of woman I am. You're very confusing, Mr. Lee—Jack. I—I don't know what to make of anything at all. Yesterday I was—well, it was pretty terrible. And now all of a sudden you've got me twirling around in circles. Where *is* your daughter? And why do you have that silly grin on your face?"

"The grin is pure enjoyment," he chuckled. "I need to keep you confused, lady. As for my daughter, she's waiting for this." His hand fumbled with the ring on the steering wheel, and a deep-throated horn sounded. Almost at once Nora popped out the door and ran for the car.

"It *is* all right?" Jack asked softly.

"Of course it is," she returned gently. "But you didn't have to go through all this con game. I would have done it for *Nora* in any case."

"Hey, how about that? Just for Nora." His injured innocence was too much to stand. She burst into giggles.

"Is this some game you and your daughter play very often?"

"Nope. This is the first performance." He turned the key, and the big motor sprung into life.

"The act could use a little more polish," she said primly, and then, to emphasize the point, moved to the far side of the seat. "Why don't you sit up front here, Nora, between your dad and I?"

The invitation was accepted with alacrity. The child wiggled her way over the back of the seat and plumped herself down between the two of them, her hair flying, and her smile glowing. It just matched the brilliance of the sun, breaking through the valley haze at last. "And just where do you propose we go to eat these sandwiches, Mr. Lee?"

"Oh, me, back to Mr. Lee?"

"Don't eat the sandwiches," Nora whispered in her ear.

"I have remarkably good hearing," her father interjected.

"For a man your age," the girl returned, giggling. "That's what Grandma always said."

Katie was caught on the horns of a dilemma. She wanted to know about the sandwiches because her stomach was growling. But even more she wanted to know about "Grandma." Or anything and everything about this crazy family beside her. Family. How's that for a nice word? My daughter and I—and—him? Dreamer! As usual, her thoughts crossed on separate tracks and she lost the point she was trying to make. "Does your grandmother like sandwiches?" she asked.

"Not these sandwiches," Nora hissed at her. "He bought them two nights ago at a fast food place on the road! Ptomaine Heaven, I think it was."

"You mean your father lied to me?" Katie overemphasized the dramatic. The phrase came out sounding like a line from the ancient thriller, *East Lynne*.

"Never," her father interrupted. "Truth also lies in the eye of the beholder, and is subject to a certain amount of—manipulation."

"What he means is——" Nora started off.

"I know what he means," Katie laughed.

"And no, her grandmother doesn't exactly care for sandwiches," he added. "Does that take care of everything?"

"Everything but my stomach and my job," she sighed. "I think I'd better check the job first. The kindergarten is next to the Presbyterian church, and the library is just around the corner. Could you drive me there and drop me off? I'll only be a minute. This is my day off from both, but I don't know when either of them wants me tomorrow."

"And then?" He looked at her over his daughter's head. That little suspicion—that doubt—was in his eyes again. What did it remind her of? Papa, with his fishing line in the creek, and not really sure he had hooked his fish?

She gulped at the thought. "And then——" she stuttered. "Then I think we can all go home and I'll make us a lunch—and—and we'll see."

"Free lunch, Pop," the little girl squealed. "Cooked by somebody who really knows how to cook! You do, don't you, Katie?"

"Cook? Oh, yes, that's one of my few talents. Nothing fancy, mind you."

"Thank heaven," the child bubbled. "Daddy can't cook for a nickel, and neither can Grandma, and every time she fires a—oh my, I wasn't supposed to mention that, was I? Oh, Katie, you are going to be the salvation of our family. Is that the right word, Dad?"

"That's the right word, love. The very right word. Is this the church?"

"I'll just be a minute," Katie bubbled. It was contagious, being with this crazy pair. What was the name of that fellow you were going to marry? Don't remember, do you? Good for you, girl, you're finally getting a little sense. You've mourned the best part of a year, and now it's time to get about the world's business!

In the event, it took less time than even she had thought, and she came out of the building with a very sober face.

"Oh-oh," Jack murmured as he came around the car to help her in. "Now what?"

"I—I lost my job," she mumbled. "They—the Board fired me."

"For what reason?"

"You know," she sighed. "Because I wasn't found not guilty. Drugs and kids don't mix, I guess. But I need that job. I *need* it."

"Right now what you need is a good meal," he commanded. "To hell with the school—and the library, too." The car spurted forward, giving her hardly time to fasten her seat belt. The little girl between them moved closer to her.

"Daddy only talks like that when he's mad," she whispered. "Look at his eyebrows and his eyelashes." Katie peeped out of the corner of her eyes. Their driver was concentrating on something. The road, perhaps. His eyebrows were perfectly straight, his lashes half closed, and his lips were moving.

"That's a sure sign?" she whispered back.

"Sure sign," the little girl agreed. "Somebody around here is gonna get in a lot of trouble—real soon."

"I hope it's not me."

"Oh, it's not you. He likes you. He likes you a whole lot. So do I."

"That's nice." Katie picked up one of the little hands and squeezed it. "I—I like you, too. But I think two of the three of us are plumb crazy."

"Maybe all three," the man slouched behind the wheel contributed. He drove on for another few minutes, his lips twitching like fury. And then, almost as if he was talking to himself, "That was a very silly case. Why did they charge you rather than Filmore? They had nothing at all to connect you with the case——"

"Except that he was in my house," Katie interjected.

"Not important," he continued. "They would have to connect you to him or you to the drugs... or do you suppose that was what Filmore offered them? To connect you to the drugs?"

"But I never—I don't think I've met this Filmore boy more than once in my whole life."

"Funny, isn't it?" he repeated. "It almost seemed that the prosecutor and the deputy were out to get you, by any means, while the judge was all on your side of things. How does that come about?"

"The old and the new," she told him. "The judge isn't really my uncle, but he and my family, and, oh, about forty percent of the people in the village, we've all been here for centuries, so to speak. On the other hand there are new people—folks who've just moved into the area, like the Fessendens and the prosecutor and the Lesters—and the sheriff is new, too. Latecomers. New money, that sort of thing. They're trying to take over the town, and the old order is resisting. But I don't know what they'd want with me. I'm just a very small cog in the wheel around here, you know."

He drove on for another few minutes, and then started muttering again. "But you have something," he stated. "You have that fine house and all those acres around it. Now who would want your house—or your acres?"

"Nobody that I know of," she sighed. "I've been trying to—I've been debating about selling, but there aren't a lot of buyers in these parts. What are you thinking?"

"Nothing much," he commented as they came up on the house. "But there's an old Roman instruction in curious cases like this. *Cui bono?*" He nodded his head and left the Latin phrase hanging there, as if she certainly ought to know what it meant. And I'm darned if I'm going to embarrass myself by admitting my ignorance, she told herself firmly.

Nora came to her pride's aid. "What's that mean, Dad?" the little girl asked. "Cui watchamacallit?"

"Cui bono?" her father repeated in very satisfied tones. "Who profits from it?"

CHAPTER FOUR

"LOVELY," Jack said warmly, pushing his chair back. He was looking at the ruins of what once had been lunch. Thick slices of rare roast beef, warmed with her special gravy recipe, baked potatoes from her only extravagance—a fine Microwave unit—spinach out of the freezer, and a tossed salad.

"You didn't care for the salad?" she asked tentatively.

"Well, you were eating it, so I thought not to crowd you," he chuckled. "To tell the truth I'm basically a meat and potato man That's a hard thing to be, living in Washington, and eating out all the time."

"Yeah," Nora complained. "While I had to stay home with Grandma and eat that *French* stuff." Her tone indicated that French cooking had come out last in the cuisine race. And then she confirmed it. "I like peanut butter and jelly." The child looked over at her begging to have the delicacy produced instantly.

"Next time," Kate half promised. "But you have to eat some vegetables."

"Daddy doesn't."

"But he will. Honestly he will."

Her father failed to look enthusiastic about the whole idea. In fact he shook his head negatively until he read Katie's frown, and suddenly became interested in the leftover apple pie.

"You don't see much of this in the big city," he remarked.

"Well, there's plenty in the valley," she said, doing her best to restrain laughter. "You can have any kind of pie you want in these parts, as long as it's apple. Now why don't you two scoot and select which bedroom you want, while I wash up the dishes?''

"That shouldn't take long. Nora and I will help.'' The pair of them stood up simultaneously, and began to pile dishes in the dishwasher in the corner of the big kitchen. Another relic from the good old days. And I have to spoil their fun!

''I regret to tell the pair of you that the dishwasher doesn't work.'' She walked over behind them. Jack immediately had his head into the insides.

''Doesn't work?'' It was some sort of rhetorical statement, not a question. He checked the power cord, reseating it into the plug in the wall, closed the lid, and pressed the start button. ''Everything seems to work fine, lady.''

''Did I tell you my dad is a great fixer?'' Nora was trying to make some sort of point. ''He's terrible handy to have around the house.'' What's this child trying to do to me—to us? Katie asked herself. And because she was afraid she knew the answer she blushed and closed her ears.

''I don't see a thing wrong with it,'' he repeated. Katie shook her head wryly. A crazy pair.

''Test the water,'' she suggested. He looked at her, puzzled, then lifted up the lid and dipped a finger into the barrel of the washer.

''Nothing wrong with the water,'' he reported. His daughter tugged at his shirt.

''It's supposed to be hot,'' she offered in a conspiratorial whisper.

''Oh, hot! There's something wrong with the hot water?''

"There's nothing wrong with it," Kate said primly. "There just isn't any."

"Ah." His whole face lighted up, like Sherlock Holmes hot on the trail. "Tell me about it."

"Tell you about it? I—I have to think about that. Why don't you two go select your bedrooms while I do the dishes and think?"

"Nora, do you get the idea that she's trying to get rid of us?"

"Yup. We better go."

"Oh, and there's no heat," she told them. "So if you take a bedroom up on the third floor it's pretty cold up there."

"No hot water, no heat?" he probed. She made a face at him.

"This isn't a hotel, you know."

"C'mon, Dad. Don't tease."

"Why, baby—what a thing to say about your dad!"

The little girl stamped her foot. "Don't tease, Dad. I don't want this one to get away!" Her father considered for a moment, and then a broad grin spread across his face. "What a lovely thought," he mused. "You are indeed your father's daughter." They tumbled out of the kitchen together, leaving a completely confused woman behind them.

For some time after that, while she heated a pan of water and struggled with the dishes, Katie could hear the pair of them racing around upstairs. The house was solidly built, but a hundred and fifty years of hard usage had warped a floor plank here and there, and sounds reverberated in every direction. Carpets, that's what I need. Carpets, a new roof, a new furnace, enough money to pay off all the bills. And there are only twenty-nine days left in April.

On any other day this past year that last thought would have thrown her into a panic, but now there was too much happiness around for her to be down for more than a minute or two. And then there was only one pair of footsteps upstairs, and some heavy body was climbing down into the cellar. Where I haven't been in ages, she reminded herself. Dad always had a man who came for things in the cellar.

"And if you were of any use to yourself," she lectured aloud, "you would have found out about things in the cellar, instead of floating around trying to be a social butterfly, without a penny to fly on!"

"Wow!" Nora said from the door. "You're a butterfly? Pretty big for a butterfly."

"Snooping?" she returned, but in a friendly tone.

"That's the only way to learn anything," the girl said. "Can I help?"

"Well—yes. What else does your father like to eat besides roast beef?"

"Good-looking girls," Jack Lee said from out in the hall. "I have to go back to that hardware store for a control valve and a length of pipe and a couple of new nipples."

"Do you really?" Katie was not about to take the ultimate step and ask what and why.

"Go away," his daughter instructed him. "This is woman-talk."

"I should be so lucky," he laughed. "Between the pair of you I suspect there isn't enough knowledge about woman-talk to put in a thimble." Katie had a blockbuster of a comment to throw at him, but before she could get her tongue in gear he was gone. So she stuck it out at his disappearing back.

Nora picked up the dishcloth to wipe, looking the industrious well-trained little girl. Which she might be, but having a father like that—well, who knows? "Katie, do you have a boyfriend?"

"I—no, I guess not. I didn't get all the gravy spots off that dish. Let me have it back."

"This one? I meant—you don't have no attractions at all."

"*Any* attractions, dear. Any. We don't say *no*."

"No, I suppose we don't. I'm glad."

"Why? Because that's the last of the dishes? Now, what do you think your father would like for tonight?"

"Peanut butter and jelly?"

"I doubt that. How about fish? I've got a nice fillet of haddock. You like fish?"

"Sure." A very subdued answer. The sort one gets from children who were trying very hard to maintain good relations without poisoning themselves.

"And three kinds of vegetables?" A malicious jab at a poor, undeserving child! It's her father you're aiming at, not Nora!

"I don't care. Like Daddy says, I can take them or leave them alone. Mostly leave them alone."

"This isn't getting us anywhere," Katie laughed. "Come on, help me find the sheets and things and get the beds made."

It was a surprise to find that Nora hadn't chosen the small bedroom at the top of the house. Instead she had picked the room next to Katie's, separated by a shared bathroom. "And your dad?"

There was a large familiar grin on the child's face as she turned in the other direction. "This one." She threw open the door of the bedroom directly across the hall, the big master bedroom which took up almost half of the south wing.

"Why do you suppose he picked this one, Nora?"

"Because the bed's so big, that's why. Where are the sheets?"

It took almost an hour to find everything, all carefully put away in camphor balls, and needing a little airing that time would not allow.

By that time Jack was back, roaring up to the house in a cloud of dust. The two girls went downstairs to greet him, but he had already plunged into the cellar, and was banging on miscellaneous pipes, making odd noises, cursing a time or two, and, at last, giving himself a cheer.

"Hey, up there," he yelled up the stairs. "Turn one of the thermostats up to seventy degrees." Katie went back into the living room and performed the simple adjustment. There was a clanking and groaning from the cellar, things started, motors ran, and the lawyer sauntered up the stairs. His face was smeared on one side with soot, both hands and arms were filthy, but he was grinning that great big grin.

"You fixed something?"

"Dad fixes everything," Nora said indignantly. "Only in Grandma's house she won't let him."

He gave the child a warning glance, and she covered her mouth with her hand.

"A prophet without honor?" Katie was finding it hard not to smile back at him, and this was a serious time. "What was the problem?"

"The feed pipe from your oil tank broke. You have a safety valve that shut down and turned everything off. All I had to do was replace the pipe and the safety valve, clean up the mess, and there we are. Your hot-water tank is a part of your furnace. A real old installation. You should have called a plumber. How come you didn't?"

"It's not that easy," she sighed. "It's a long trip from town, and plumbers keep office hours these days." And then, much more softly, "And they don't come when they know they can't get paid."

"Money?"

"I—yes. But there was more than that. After all, it was getting to be spring, and I didn't know about the hot water, and there's only—well. There just isn't much time left, and——"

"Hey, now. You've been doing fine all day. No more tears. Want to tell me about it?"

She shook her head. "I—I have to start the dinner."

He pulled her over to the sofa and sat her down. "You'd be a lot better off if you told me about it," he said softly. One of his arms came around her shoulders. Nora had quietly effaced herself. He tilted Katie's chin up in the right direction. And if he kisses me I'll blow all to pieces, she told herself. All to pieces. His mouth came down gently in her direction. She steeled herself, hoping that she had enough strength to stay afloat during the encounter. But just as she decided she hadn't, and could therefore surrender with honor, there was a tremendous series of banging noises from all over the house. The living room rocked with the noise, and then with the echoes. The whole house seemed to shake on its foundation.

Nora came rushing back into the room, frightened. Her father reluctantly disengaged himself, and stood up. His lips were moving silently.

"Daddy?"

"Nothing to worry about," he sighed. "Hot-water radiators?"

"Yes," Katie told him. "One in every room. Two in the dining room and the study. Twenty-two rooms. What's the matter?"

"Oh, Lord," he returned. "I had to drain the hot-water pipes before I could solder a new section in. And when you turn on the water again there's a great deal of air in the pipes. Every single one of those radiators had a petcock on the top to let air out. And that's what we have to do, go around the house and let the air out of each one of the radiators. Mount up, troops."

"I've got to fix the dinner," Katie interjected hastily.

"I don't know what a petcock is," Nora added dolefully. He looked at them both sternly.

"Desertion in the face of the enemy," he charged, then grinned, and dashed out of the room to do his duty.

"Did you get kissed, Katie?" the child asked as she watched her father take off on the run.

"No, darn it." Well, it was an honest answer, she told herself. I really was prepared for total surrender. "Come on, kid, let's go wrestle with the fish."

The rest of the afternoon was slow and lazy, as Katie and Nora got better acquainted in the kitchen, and Jack Lee dashed around the house like a cavalry trooper riding to the rescue. At four o'clock everything seemed to slow down to a stop. The two girls went out to the front stoop and sat down, to be joined shortly by Nora's wide-smiling father. "Best afternoon I've had in months," he boasted as he took a pull at the can of beer in his hand.

"We *do* have glasses," Katie said mildly.

"Never touch the things," he chuckled. "I like this. How about you, baby?"

"I'm not a baby," Nora returned with considerable dignity. "It's all wonderful." She gestured out in front of her, to the westward, where the long flat top of

Massanutten held the sun up in the sky, and then behind them, where the Blue Ridge and Mount Marshall towered. "I sure do like this place, Dad. We oughta stay in a town like this." It was a soft, wistful appeal. Kate slipped an arm around the little girl's thin shoulders and offered comfort in a light squeeze. The child shifted her weight and fell back against Kate's breast—and sighed contentedly.

"Don't ham it up," her father warned. "It's all very nice. All of it. And only what—sixty miles from Washington?"

"Just about. But the roads don't exactly go straight from here to there. They tend to slant northward, toward Winchester."

"Is that a fact?" he mused. Little emotions were coursing over his face, as if he had just found another piece of a puzzle. And then he stood up. "Almost three hours to sunset?" he inquired.

"About that. Seven o'clock more or less is when we lose the sun." The clock in the living room took that as a cue and bonged off six loud chimes.

"Good Lord." Jack jumped up as if there was some rush to life, then looked at his wristwatch. "Your darn clock is two hours fast," he commented.

"No," she countered. "My darn clock is exactly on time. But the darn...bonger—it's off. What's the problem?"

He grinned and settled back against the solid post that held up the roof of the veranda. "I suspect we might have visitors tonight, ladies. One last attempt to scare you off, Miss Katie."

"You'll never make a Southern accent," she laughed. "Oh, the dinner!" She jumped up and ran for the kitchen. He came along behind her. Nora remained on the step, trying to identify the flocks of birds that wheeled overhead.

"So you don't care for my Rhett Butler impersonation?"

"Not without a great deal more practice," she teased. "Most of the strong dialects in the United States are fading away—within the big cities, that is. Sooner or later, my professors always said, there will be a standard American spoken in these United States."

"Your professors?"

"You didn't think it possible?" she laughed as she checked the oven's heat and slid the tray of fillets in. "I was a student at the University of Virginia for two and a quarter years. I hardly believe it myself. Nobody could be as stupid as I've been these last nine months. Everything seems to be falling to pieces around my head, and I don't know why!" She turned back to him and stood there, hands on hips. "Why, Mr.—er—Jack? Why?"

"Well, I hardly know what's happened, so I can't tell you all the 'whys,'" he said softly. "You have to confide in me, Kate. Talk it all out."

Her hands were busy with the salad. The rice was bubbling nicely. Her mind wandered off through the months. He was a good man, this Jack Lee. That's what Papa would have called him. A good man. You could almost say it was written on his shirt collar. So why not tell him? Perhaps not everything, but something.

"We were a happy family," she sighed. "My dad had money—family money. My mother had some, too. But they loved each other so much there wasn't room for me." She paused and grimaced at the memory.

"And we had this farm. Two hundred and forty acres, with twenty acres under tobacco allocations. You know about that?"

"A federal subsidy." He nodded his head. "Worth its weight in gold. You can lease the rights out to other farmers."

"No," she said angrily. "No." He shrugged his shoulders.

"So then tell me about it."

"We—my mother died four years ago," she continued. "It was an accident. Can you imagine that? She was run down by a car out on the county road." And I'm not going to cry, she told herself fiercely. I've cried all I'm going to! "She never told me she loved me, and I never told her—I loved her, and suddenly it was all too late, and she was gone." His head snapped up. She had not meant to say it aloud—it just came out. She crammed her fist into her mouth as if to shut off the flow of words. But he was not about to let her escape.

He crossed that invisible boundary that she maintained as her private territory, and hugged her. The warmth was her undoing. The fist came loose and the words tumbled out. "They wanted a boy," she mumbled. "Or maybe a nice, cuddly little girl, like Mama. And I wasn't either of those things. So they put up with me— but left me outside their little circle. I was the cuckoo in the nest. I tried so hard to be like Mama, but she was only five foot two, with dark black hair. And Dad, he was only five feet seven. They—just didn't know what to make of me."

"And how did you cope?"

"I—I just sort of tried to shrink, but I was too awkward. So Dad tried his best to make me into a boy. But after I—after my twelfth birthday that didn't work, so they sent me off to school. That's the way it went. Home for a week, then off to some other school or camp—until Mama died."

"And then?"

"And then Papa went to pieces. He really needed me, you know. So I came home, but he—when Mama died he lost all his interests. Except gambling. He never lost that. And then, nine months ago, he died. He died of lung cancer. The first thing I did after the funeral was to go out and have that entire tobacco allotment plowed under. Twenty acres of tobacco. I replaced it with soy beans. I don't ever intend to grow that—that weed again. No matter how badly I need the money!"

"Well," he said cautiously. "Well, well."

And that's how interesting my life story is, she told herself bitterly. Well, well. He can't think of a thing to say. Look at him, his brows all furrowed, his eyes blank. He's a hundred miles away. I wonder where his wife is?

She paid for her own wanderings. Not looking where she was moving, her hands landed on the hot edge of the fish tray. Her scream was more of disgust than pain. The pan teetered in the mouth of the open oven, and then fell on the floor. Upside-down, of course, her mind confirmed. Her burnt fingers had gone to her mouth, just meeting the tears rolling down her cheeks. "I—I don't know what I'm doing," she quavered, and then bit off the words. They weren't really necessary. Anyone could see she had lost her marbles.

"I do," he said, gathering her up like a bundle of laundry and hustling her over to the sink. The cool water was a blessing.

"I—I'm all right. It was only a little burn. You could put me down—please?"

His face was so close to hers it filled her whole horizon. Late afternoon, she thought, and he already needs another shave. I wonder if he would have a curly beard? There was a scent about him, too—a scent of man, untainted by after-shave and perfumes. Real man. Why am I so alive to his every move?

"You really need to keep that finger out of the kitchen for a while," he said as he let her feet slip slowly toward the floor. Katie had the feeling of *déjà vu*. She slid down the length of him, just as she had while in the apple tree, feeling the strength, the purpose, the wild sexuality of him. Her face was as red as her two fingers when she stood on her own feet and readjusted her clothing. He was still standing close—too close for comfort. He isn't doing anything, her conscience yelled at her. He's just standing there! Wild sexuality? Where did you get that crazy idea?

It was her own desperate need to break the tension that caused her to move away. Her feet went slowly, leadenly. "Oh, my, the dinner!" she exclaimed, her voice cracking under the strain. "The dinner's ruined."

"We couldn't just pick it up and wash it off?" he inquired from behind her. Which made her miss the laughter in his eyes.

"No, of course not," she almost shouted at him. "What sort of a—housekeeper do you think I am?" She scurried over to the oven and began to restore a little order. To her *mind*, not to the floor and oven. What sort of a *housewife* do you think I am? That was the phrase that she had swallowed down, almost choking on it. What's wrong with your words, Katie Lovewell? What is it?

You've been asleep for nine months, and now every time this man comes around there are rockets going off in your stupid head!

"Hey, let me do that before you really mess things up." His big hands picked her up from her knees and set her aside as if she were about his daughter's size.

"Nora!" The bellow was loud enough to be heard in Front Royal—or Winchester! The child came running in, a big smile on her face.

"Nora, our landlady has burned her hand. Scoot up to the bathroom and see if you can find some Solarcane to put on her fingers."

"In *our* bathroom," Katie added. The girl dimpled and ran. The father took hold of both of Katie's elbows and backed her into one of the kitchen chairs.

"Sit there," he ordered, and began to clear up the mess for himself.

"Bossy," she muttered under her breath.

"You'd better believe it." He chuckled as he worked. "If Nora and I were out camping we'd just brush this fish off and have it. Where the devil is the garbage can?"

"I—I haven't swept the floor in a week," she mumbled.

"Is that so?" There was a big lint ball in the dustpan he had found behind the door. The pain in her fingers had become small potatoes.

"Are you laughing at me?"

"Not in the least," he commiserated. "I wouldn't dream of laughing at a lady in pain."

"Then how come it sounds so strange when you say it?"

"Must be my Slavic accent," he suggested. But he turned his back as he said it, then Nora erupted into the kitchen with the tube of balm, and her chance to get back at him had passed.

"So what will we have for dinner?" she asked the pair of them as they cleaned and polished her kitchen far beyond the need created by the dropped fish.

"I've been gaining a little weight lately," he said. That solemn tone again. The lawyer tone, she told herself grimly. As if his next question would be, "And when did you stop beating your wife?"

"So perhaps it wouldn't hurt us all to fast?" she asked. "We—we could always go out to eat. There are two nice little restaurants in Stanfield...my treat." And I haven't the slightest idea where I'd get the money, she thought. My credit card's exhausted, and I haven't a—good Lord, of course I have! There's the fifty-dollar bill I got from Mrs. Fessenden! Her face brightened visibly as the suggestion became a real possibility.

"You know, Katie, you have a wonderful face," Jack said. Her head came up suspiciously, as it always did when someone tried to pay her a compliment. And then he stepped on her ego. "Anyone can read just what you're thinking by watching your face!"

She did her best to school herself. Calm dignity, her mind recited. Calm dignity. Or hit him one! He must have seen *that* thought too—he stepped back a pace or two, grinning.

"In any event, we can't go tonight." He looked down to check his wristwatch. "I'm expecting company."

"I could make the dinner," Nora interjected. Katie looked down at her, surprised. Eight years old? I can make the dinner? And her father doesn't seem to be the least put out by it all.

"Good idea," he commented. "I've some things to see to outside. Katie, one of the things you should know is that there's only room for one cook at a time in the kitchen. So you go putter around upstairs while Nora makes a spread for us. Right?"

"Now you tell me," she grumbled. "If it hadn't been for you haunting my kitchen we wouldn't be in this mess." He and his daughter both grinned at her, and he gave her the big finger pointing at the kitchen door, the way a baseball umpire indicated a player or manager who'd been thrown out of the game. The ridiculousness of the whole affair seeped up into Katie's front brain cells. She shrugged her shoulders at them, and walked off.

There was always something to do in such a big house, of course, but her good intentions all went down the drain when she went into her bathroom and found that the hot water gushed and steamed on application. More to hide her transgression than anything else she locked herself into the bathroom, filled the tub, and took her first leisurely soak in many a day.

She was back downstairs by six, urged on by a call from Nora. The table in the kitchen was set for three; her "tenants" were waiting for her. Jack stood up and held her chair for her. It was something she was not accustomed to. She sank into it like a duchess, prepared for almost anything except the peanut butter sandwich in the center of her plate. She looked up at them both. That calm stare came back to her from their separate eyes. A look of challenge, anticipation, laughter. And I can play the game, she told herself, squaring her shoulders and sitting back deep in the chair.

"Lovely," she said. "Chunky? I always like chunky peanut butter."

"Well, now," Nora confessed. And then more brightly, "But it's got apple butter in it, too." There was a little anxiety in the statement.

"That's fine," she giggled. "I—apple is the Holy Word in these parts. I just love apple butter!" The little girl chortled and relaxed. The dinner went on, with more conversation than consumption.

"And there's seconds of everything," Nora added as her father pushed back his chair and began to stack the dishes.

"No—no, thank you." The child had come around to Kate's chair, expectantly. "I don't think I can eat another morsel." Without thinking about it at all, her arm went around the child's shoulders and enveloped her in a warm hug. It felt so comforting—and yet so ordinary. It was something that *ought* to be done, she told herself.

They adjourned to the front porch, bringing their coffee cups with them. The western sky was bright with promise for the morrow. "'Red skies at night, sailors' delight,'" she quoted.

"Sailors? Around these parts?"

"Well, we have more rivers than we know what to do with," she staunchly defended. "And plenty of lakes and things. You don't have to be on the ocean to be a sailor, you know."

"Of course not." He had gone into that absent-minded shell again. A sudden and complete transition. After a few minutes of silence he asked, "Any lakes on your property?"

"Why, no. Why do you ask?"

"Nothing really. I suppose your land runs in back of the house?"

She shook her head in the gathering dusk. "No, of course not. It's all in front of us. It runs right up to Route 340."

"Ah." The conversation died. The little girl was yawning.

"What time do you go to bed, Nora?"

"At eight o'clock—sometimes nine. Whenever Dad—when we can be together." The living-room clock struck eleven behind them.

"Then it's time for bed," Katie said. "Can I take you up?"

"And tell me a story?"

"And tell you a story."

"My dad can't tell stories for beans."

"That's difficult to believe," Katie chuckled. "I thought *all* lawyers were good at telling stories. But yes, I know a story or two. I'm a librarian."

He always seemed to catch the tail end of statements. "How did you get to be a librarian?" he asked. And looked as if he really wanted to know.

"At the university," she returned. "I majored in Library Science. Come on, Nora."

"Just a minute." He held up his hand, his head cocked in a listening position. "I want the house to look just the way it did when you were alone," he finally said, in a soft, firm voice. "No more lights than usual, Katie. And make it a long story. Don't come down until I call you. Got it?"

"I——" She wanted to argue, but there was something about the way he was standing, half crouched, intense, that stopped her. And then she noticed something else. His car was gone from in front of the house, and it looked almost as if someone had swept up its tracks in the dirt of the drive. But perhaps that's an illusion, she told herself as she clutched at Nora's hand and tugged her up. Maybe it's just too dark. She turned around to say something else to Jack, but he was gone.

Child bathing was a new experience. Katie knew all about children outside their homes. How they reacted in crowds, what needed to be done to keep a child group active in a constructive direction. But this one-on-one in a bathtub was something entirely new, and enjoyable. The girl was a delight. With her share of tiny scars, freckles, and a mole right in the small of her back, she was animation and life in the water.

"Hey, *I've* already had a bath," Katie protested for the tenth time as more than a little water splashed up at her. "What a lovely mole, Nora."

"Oh, that old thing!" The girl twisted and turned, trying to observe. "That's a family thing. Grandma has one, and you should see Daddy's. His is a little lower than mine, though."

I should see Daddy's mole? That will be the day! Katie was giggling as she held up the big bath towel and the little girl stepped out on to the bath mat.

"Why do you turn all red like that?" The girl was staring at her face, her lips puckered in a need to know. All of which increased Katie's coloration.

"It's—it's the steam," she stuttered. "The bathroom's warm, and I'm not used to it."

"Yeah, well, how about that story?"

She looked like a doll in the long cotton nightgown. "I have a nightgown just like that," Katie told the girl as she dried the long blond hair with a vigorous application of toweling. "Even to the little red rosebuds on the shoulders."

"My dad bought it for me," Nora returned. "Story time?"

"In my bed," Katie suggested. "Your father said not to put on any lights in unusual places." The little girl squeaked in delight and wiggled by, out into the bedroom. The big bed became a trampoline as she bounced three times, high in the air, and then collapsed.

"That bed's pretty old," Katie advised as she stripped down the covers and managed to trap the little nymph. "It could collapse, you know."

"Aw, it can hold me," Nora returned. "I'm only nine."

"Nine? I thought you were—it doesn't matter. Now, have you ever heard the story of the Four Bears?"

"That's Three Bears," the child returned. "Once upon a time——"

"Well, in *my* story it's Four Bears," Katie said, tucking the sheets up around those bony shoulders. "Do you want to hear it or not?"

"Well, of course I do." The child settled herself against the pillows, and the story began. They had hardly progressed to the point where the Four Bears were chasing Rod Red Hood around the kitchen table, when the cars came.

The motors were like a dose of reality in a pleasant world of fantasy. Katie held a cautionary finger across the child's lips, then went over to the window and peeped out from behind the protection of the lace curtain. A bright moon lit the front yard. The cars—three of them—looked ominous in the silvery light of the moon. Three cars, one with the front doors open. And a banging on the front door.

"I want to talk to you, Katie," a voice yelled up. "I know you're up there."

"Yeah, we just want to talk," another voice commented from the cars, and a gale of laughter followed. The door shook in its sills as the knocks became blows. "Katie! You'd better let us in, lady."

"Yeah, lady!" Again the laughter from the other vehicles. And then a greater surprise. From out of the darkness behind them a bullhorn cleared its mechanical throat.

"All right, you people in the cars. We've got you surrounded. If anyone makes a wrong move, we shoot!"

Kate, her heart in her mouth, fumbled her way back to the bed. The little girl was laughing. "That's only Daddy playing cops and robbers," she giggled.

"Well——" Katie could find nothing to say. She sank down on to the bed, holding hands with the child, and drawing courage from the little girl! That was when the shots began.

It wasn't a single shot, but rather a fusillade that rocked the area, and brought screams from the passengers in the cars. The sounds seemed to be coming from the front of the house, and then from both sides. The yells from the group in front of the house were confused. Whoever had been standing on the porch made a mad dash back to his vehicle. Motors roared, and the three automobiles sprayed dust and gravel as their tires spun, caught, and roared out on to the highway.

"Oh, my God," Katie half screamed. "Your father!" She was all the way down the stairs before the import of what she was doing sank through her confused mind. I hate guns and shooting. I'm afraid of bullets! So what am I doing running like this? Because of him?

The argument served only to blind her further to what was going on. She slammed open the front door with anxious haste, and took the first three steps down off the veranda like a world-class sprinter. There was no need to go farther.

Jack came strolling up out of the dark, that broad grin on his face, trailing a handful of something in one hand. Those big arms opened, snatched her up off the ground, whirled her around, and hugged her close.

"I don't think that particular crowd will be back, ever," he chortled just before he kissed her. The world, already confused, crumbled into little pieces. She hung in his arms like a huge rag doll, unable to associate time and place and sensation, and unwilling to try. All the universe applauded. When he released her she staggered, her legs unable to support her. He rectified the problem.

"Did I scare *you*?" he asked. She could see the worried look on his face. For me, that worry, she told herself. God help me, he worries about *me*!

"It's you I'm worried about," she yelled at him, suddenly angry. "You—you might have been killed out there! You have to take more care, because——" Because if you don't, I'll never be able to glue myself back together again. Never! Her mind prepared the words, but her tongue was unwilling to release them.

"You——"

"Hey," he said, alarmed at her confusion. "There were only five of them."

"It wasn't the *them*," she screamed at him. "You could have been hurt badly—with all those—who was it out there with——?" The words stuck in her throat. She threw herself hungrily at him, hanging on desperately around his neck while her lips did their best to devour him. He was startled at first, but then caught the spirit of the game, and joined in. They didn't break until, out of breath, they heard Nora at the upstairs window.

"If you two keep that up all night I'll never hear the end of my story," the little girl yelled down.

"Yeah, story," her father panted.

"You could have been shot!" Katie repeated breathlessly.

"Me?" The look on his face was pure astonishment. "Not with these." He held up the string of firecrackers in her face. "Half the damn things didn't even go off. I'm never going to buy firecrackers in Maryland again. Never again!"

"Firecrackers," she gasped. "Why, you——"

"Uh-uh, Katie Lovewell," he said as he held both her hands to protect himself. "Southern ladies don't use words like that!"

"I never said a word," she gasped as she struggled to free herself.

"No, but you were thinking them!"

And I was, she told herself as the struggle ceased. And it was for sure. Darn the man!

He was standing close, and in the light of the early moon she could see the planes and shadows of his rugged face. And his heavy black eyebrows. Black, except for the tiny tuft over the center of each eye—a tiny white tuft that went straight up, almost like the Devil's horns in medieval paintings. An omen, she asked herself? Am I dealing with Beelzebub himself, or just a facsimile?

A look of complete frustration settled on his face as she giggled at her own imagination!

CHAPTER FIVE

ON THE next bright morning Kate did the one thing she hardly ever did. She slept late. The morning sun was already high over the Blue Ridge. A clock was booming—eleven times. Her mind filtered the sound, translated, and spurred her up out of the warm bed.

She bounced up and over to the half-opened window, and inhaled the mixture of sweetness and bird song. For some reason it seemed wonderful to be alive on this particular morning. She made a quick stab at her usual exercises, but as she moved through the graceful drill her mind recalled the previous night, and her mood changed. The nerve of that man!

There was hot water at the shower head. She reveled in it, working up her anger as hard as she worked up a lather. When her conscience forced her out of the shower she was ready to assault the world.

Ghengis Khan, she told herself grimly as she threw on a T-shirt and wraparound skirt. That's what he's going to think I am when I get through with him. Imagine the nerve of that man! He had no right to frighten me so! Katie started for the stairs, but had second thoughts. Just because you mean to chew him up and spit him out doesn't mean you shouldn't look nice.

So back to her dressing table, the silver-mounted brushes that had been her father's last gift to her, and a massive attack on her tumbled hair. I really ought to get it cut, she sighed, but knew she never would. Under the brush strokes order was restored. She fastened it into a ponytail with a little pink ribbon. It made her look young, and she wanted to be young this day. Young and angry. Anything else would be overdoing it. I'm only going to breakfast with the man! And that was the crusher—breakfast with the man. Just to be on the safe side she added the tiniest dab of perfume. Barely a touch.

Her slippers were the slide-in style. The heels bumped on each step as she clattered down to the kitchen. The two Lees were there already, the father staring into his second mug of coffee, the little girl finishing up her scrambled eggs with such enthusiasm.

"Oh-oh," Nora said. Her father looked up. "Storm warning," the girl told him as she snatched up her glass of orange juice and faded out of the line of fire. Katie jerked a chair out from under the table and threw herself into it with reckless abandon.

"Well?" She stared at him with daggers in her eyes.

"Well, what?" A cautious approach, as he felt his way.

"Well, what did the child mean by all that mumbo jumbo?"

"That—ah—sailor talk? You're a sailor, aren't you?"

"You know darn well I'm not! What did she mean?"

He squirmed a little, then set his mug down and tried to outstare her. It didn't work; her anger quotient was already set too high.

"So all right," he sighed. "It means small boat warning, storm signal. To us sailors, of course. I thought you were a sailor."

"I'm not a sailor," she snapped. "I'm just a big dumb country girl who has fallen among thieves. How *dare* you?"

"How dare I what?"

"How dare you frighten me half to death last night with your darn fire crackers. How dare you let me think you were in the midst of all that shooting. How dare you!"

"Fallen among thieves? I'm a lawyer."

"Same thing!"

"Well!" He dragged the word out. It almost served to take him around the table, where he snatched up both her hands just as she attempted to club him with one open palm. "So you really care? I thought I'd be a month getting you to that point!"

"What in the world are you babbling about? Of course I care. I mean I would——" I mean my mouth has gotten me dead into a possum trap, fool! "I mean I care about any human being caught in a terrible situation. How did I know there wasn't a Libyan hit man out there in the dark, looking for you? How could I——?"

"You needn't cry." One of his fingers trapped the falling globe of a tear. He pulled her up out of her chair. She came willingly, moving forward into the warmth, the protection that she had dreamed about all the restless long night.

"I—I'm not crying," she stammered.

"Of course not. Something in your eye, no doubt."

"Yes." Yes, yes, yes. I've got you in my eye! What a nerve you've got, insinuating yourself into my house, into my life, and making me—making me feel again. How dare you?

"I don't have a clean handkerchief." His voice was deep and soothing. She cried herself out, making a mess of his linen shirtfront, and not caring. When the storm passed she leaned back to look up at at him.

"I was worried."

"I know." A feeling of regret there, and a promise. "Sometimes I don't think ahead."

"Like a little boy," she stated flatly.

"Just so. I may never grow up."

You don't have to on my account, she wanted to scream at him. I like you the way you are! But she was having trouble with words again. His lock of hair had fallen down over one eye. She stretched a finger out and flipped it back. There was a delightful look on his face. One that...

"Katie? There's somebody on the telephone who wants to speak to you." Nora sidled halfway into the kitchen, giving her father an apologetic shrug. "I had to answer the phone, didn't I?"

"Not necessarily," he grumbled. Katie struggled just enough to break free. It was not something she *wanted* to do, it was something she *had* to do. You can hardly stand nose to nose with the child's father under her very eyes, can you? She can't help but be offended for her mother's sake!

The pair of them watched as she stalked out of the room. "How come I always come in and find you kissing her?" Nora asked.

"I didn't get that far," her father complained. "How come when I'm trying to kiss her you always walk in?"

"I should knock, huh?"

"No, love." He swept her up in his arms and hugged her mightily. "Not at all. You're the first woman in my heart."

"Hah!" his daughter said. She had learned a great deal in her few years.

"Why is it, baby, that you keep trying to marry me off to every woman I bring home?"

"Grandma keeps telling me to do that. 'Spur him on,' she keeps saying."

"Hey, they're only girlfriends."

"You don't need a girlfriend. You got me."

"So?"

"I need a mother. Grandma keeps saying so. And you're not much of a chooser. I like this one a lot."

"I—think maybe I do too, love. Where is she?"

They found Kate in the living room, slumped in a straight-backed chair by the telephone table, staring blankly out of the window.

"Katie?" Jack walked across the room quietly. For such a big man he moved like a cat. "Katie?"

She jerked her head around, looking as if she had traveled a million miles since she'd left the kitchen. There was a glisten of moisture in her eyes.

"I—I'm sorry. Did you say something?"

He put both his hands on her shoulders. "What is it?"

She waved him off, unwilling to discuss the problem. He insisted, bending down to one knee beside her and cradling her face between his hands. "What?"

"Everything—I don't know," she said dully. "I just can't understand. Everything seems to be falling apart. The library called. They've suspended me. Now I don't have a job at all, no money coming in, and hardly any time left. I—I don't understand."

"Any time to what?"

"I—I don't want to talk about it. Why is all this happening to me? Why did those—people—why did they come last night? Why was I arrested? What—I can't even hold a part-time job in a town library, and that's the only discipline in which I've been trained. What am I going to do when I have to sell the farm?"

"You didn't mention that before," he said solemnly. "Selling the farm, I mean. Hey, now." He pulled her head over toward him and kissed each of her leaking eyes. "For a girl who doesn't cry much you surely do get your eyelids wet."

"Why, Jack? Just tell me why?"

"Come over here with me," he sighed, and, without waiting for her approval, picked her up off the chair and carried her to the couch. She settled back in its corner, then leaned toward him as he joined her. Her head fell onto his shoulder as if it were her natural place. He moved a couple of times to find the comfort point, his arm around her shoulders, the other hand holding both of hers, resting in her lap.

"Nora," he called.

"I know," the little girl said from the protection of the doorway. "Go take a walk, Nora. Don't be snoopy. Nora. Well, Nora knows when she's not wanted."

"And thank God for that," he muttered into Katie's hair. "Now, little lady. You have to sell the farm?"

"Yes." She sniffled a couple of times. I'm not crying! I'm not! "Papa—gambled. When the—he left everything to me, but there wasn't anything to leave. Does that make any sense? They've been probating the will. You know about that sort of thing?"

"I know."

"At the end of this month they have to settle up the estate."

"Who is *they*?"

"Papa's lawyer. Mr. Bledsoe. Of Bledsoe & Gerney."

"That's a familiar name. Gerney. The prosecutor, wasn't he?"

"I—I hadn't thought. It's such a small district. Prosecuting is only a part-time job."

"Bledsoe & Gerney, huh? There can't be much call for a *pair* of lawyers in Stanfield."

"I guess not. They go to Winchester, Front Royal, Staunton—places like that. And they have a real estate thing going... What's the matter?"

Jack snapped to attention, and, since his arm was behind her, the movement had thrown her up against him, hard. His lips were pursing in and out. And then he settled back down again. "Nothing's wrong," he said quietly. "Just a cramp in my leg."

She looked at him suspiciously. People with cramps in their legs usually massaged the leg, or jumped up, or something of that nature. Not this one. But he *was* very adept at concocting a story.

"Go on, please. You were saying that they were settling up, and by the end of the month——?"

"Mr. Bledsoe said that without a doubt the debts would exceed the assets, and so—well, you know how badly things are going with small farms. Who would want to buy a farm these days? Maybe I might make enough to cover the debts, but then—this old house is a monster, but it's all the home I've ever had!"

"That's how you see your problem? You have to sell the farm?"

"Why, yes, what else is there?" She sat up to look at him. He was wrestling with a problem again. She could see it all on his face. Not what the problem was, but rather that he was struggling with it.

"I don't know," he said finally. "But I intend to find out. In the meantime..." Again that pursing of lips, that far-seeing stare in his eye, the tip of his tongue coming out to moisten his upper lip.

"In the meantime," he said forcefully, smiling at her, "I find that I've more business to do in these parts than

I had thought. How about this? I need a place for Nora and me to camp out, and some adult supervision for her while I'm busy. Suppose, Miss Lovewell, that I hire both you and your house for the next couple of weeks? How would that suit?"

"I—I'd be glad to help," she returned, using a finger to dry her eyes again. "But I couldn't take any money for it. It would be out of friendship."

"Nonsense," he chuckled. "Friendship doesn't stock the freezer, or pay for the oil for the furnace, nor compensate for having my very own librarian on hand. All that takes money." He named a very sizable amount that made her head spin, and then he sat there and watched her response. She hesitated, fighting with her own devils for a minute or two before capitulating.

"I—I think I could compromise my principles for a—that's a lot of money!"

"Think nothing of it," he chuckled grandly. "I'll find a way to get my money's worth. Now then, aren't there woman things to be done around here while I get about my business?" He stood up, offering her both hands. She accepted gladly, and was towed to her feet in the grand manner.

"I'm—every time I talk to you my troubles seem less important," she sighed. Perhaps he'll kiss me now? It would be such a wonderful ending to a terrible story! But he had something else in mind.

"What about laundry service?" he asked. It threw Katie completely off center.

"Laundry?"

"Yes. I can see I didn't bring enough handkerchiefs with me to survive in this house. Out you go. I have to make a telephone call. All lawyers are born with a telephone stuck in their ear."

He offered a playful little pat at her derrière as she walked out the door. His daughter poked her head in as soon as Katie disappeared into the kitchen.

"Everything okay?" she asked anxiously.

"Everything's fine," he reported. He was whistling tunelessly as he dialed a long-distance number.

"Who you calling?"

"I'm calling Uncle Vanya. Children should be seen and not heard. Why don't you go try to make a few points with our landlady?"

"Uncle Vanya? Why do we need a detective?"

"That's for me to know and you to find out," he laughed. His eyes were full of teasing love as he watched his daughter fidget in the doorway. The number was ringing. He waved the child away.

She stuck her tongue out at him. "And don't think I won't find out," she said very firmly, and headed for the kitchen.

Katie was at the kitchen stove concocting her belated breakfast when Nora came in. She was feeling much better. Unburdening helps, she thought. He can't do a thing, I'm sure, but it helps to talk. And he has such a lovely shoulder to lean on.

"Having breakfast again?"

"I'm having breakfast period," Katie commented. "I'm a big girl. I need to stoke my furnace regularly."

"You don't think you'll get fat? My aunt Helen always worries about getting fat."

"Never gave it a thought. Join me?" It was just a touch of guilty conscience. After all, she had contracted to house and feed them both, and the child looked as if she needed feeding up. Nora pulled up a chair, which seemed to signal acceptance.

"Eggs, bacon, milk?"

"Yes, ma'am."

"My, you're a polite one. Do you have a lot of aunts and uncles?"

"Ten thousand. Well—maybe not that many. We have a bunch of relatives. All in my dad's family. Do you know my uncle Vanya?"

"No, I can't say that I do. Toast, too? I meant to make biscuits, but I must have overslept. I almost never do that."

"You must be a very clever lady. You don't have any children?"

"Why, no, Nora. I'm not married."

"But you're very clever—and beautiful. You *could* be married if you wanted to."

"Why, thank you! What a nice thing to say."

"You don't want to?"

"Oh—I guess I want to," Kate mused. "Most girls think about marriage. I *almost* did get to the altar, you know, but it went sour."

"But you still want to?"

"Why are you so insistent, Nora? Yes, I suppose I want to, but a girl has to be asked, you know. I can't just pick out a good-looking man and grab him and drag him to the church."

"You could if you picked a little one," the child giggled. "I'm glad you—this is lovely milk."

And that's a quick switch of subject, Kate chuckled to herself. This one is her father's child. No doubt about that. And what's good for the goose is——

"Nora, how is it that you and your father came to this area?"

The little girl looked up at her without guile. "Oh, we were bound for Staunton, for a vacation..."

"Vacation? Aren't all the schools in session at this time of year?"

"Well——" There followed a very great hesitation, then the child's smile vanished. "Not mine," she said. "I go—I went—to a private school, and there was—well, somebody suggested why don't I go for a vacation...?"

Katie found it hard not to grin at the sincere little face which was finding it so hard to keep its own secrets. "And who was the somebody that suggested such a thing?"

"I think it was Sister Mary, the principal."

"Ah. And then what happened?"

"And then Grandma yelled at me in Croatian, and Daddy, he yelled back at her, and he just filled up the car with things, and we started for Staunton."

"But why did you stop in Stanfield?"

"You wouldn't believe. It was late at night, and dark and all, and we got a flat tire right in front of the Highway Motel, and that was it!"

"You mean your dad picked this area out because of a flat tire?"

"Yup. Do you think you'll make biscuits tomorrow?"

"And if she does, will you wash the pans?" Nora ducked away as her father came in behind her and ruffled her hair gently. He allowed no time for an answer.

"What's to see in this area, Katie? I've got some things in hand, and I think we ought to tour some of the places of interest."

"Of course," she agreed. "I'll lay out something simple for dinner—how about steaks and chips? There are a million historical sites within a fifty-mile radius of the house. The valley was one of the great battlefields of the war between the states, you know. Very educational."

"Yeah, battlefields," Nora groaned. "Is that all? More statues?"

"No." Katie shifted horses in midstream. "We could go down to the Caverns and hear the music."

"Caverns? That's more like it," the two of them chimed in.

So they put things in order, and motored in style down the Pike to Luray, then turned west on the New Market Road until they came to the Cavern parking lot, not yet crowded with the tourists that would inundate the place come high summer.

A smiling guide led their small group through the railed walkways that connected the several chambers, stopping long enough for them to hear a recitation by the Stalacpine Organ, a huge and complex arrangement that made music by striking the natural stalactites with rubber-tipped hammers. Well-lit and well patronised, the Luray Caverns were but one of the many hollows under the earth formed by years of water activity among the soft limestone rocks.

It was cool underground, cool and damp, and they were all pleased to come out into the sunshine again and make their way back to the big house. Katie felt a tug at her heart as they drove up to it; Jack was more pragmatic.

"That side gutter needs fixing!" he exclaimed. "And don't let me forget to get at that darn clock."

"You leave my clock alone," Katie insisted. "It's been that way all my life. I wouldn't know how to tell time if you fixed the thing."

"And the back door is warped," Nora reported.

"Great!" He grinned as he escorted them to the door, and then disappeared, a man with a mission that he loved. An hour later, while the two girls were working on the dinner, he was still banging busily on the back door. "See what I mean?" his daughter commented wryly. "He just loves fixing things. If we stay long enough your house will be completely overhauled. That's my daddy."

When the front doorbell rang at about four o'clock Nora ran to attend to it, and was back in a second. "He says he's Colonel Fessenden," the child reported. "He don't got——"

"Doesn't have," Katie corrected.

"Even librarians do that?" the girl asked, and then plunged back into her report. "He doesn't have a uniform or anything, so I left him in the front room."

"Oh, dear," Katie sighed. "He's a very important man in these parts. And I look a mess!"

"Not a real colonel, is he? I seen plenty of colonels in Washington. They're not all *that* important—and you look nice just the way you are. Go talk to him. I'll finish the potatoes."

"I will," Katie promised as she pulled off her apron and hung it on the hook by the kitchen door. "But first tell me how you became such a well-trained girl, love?"

Nora ducked her head and turned away to hide her mobile face. "I don't suppose you know my grandmother?"

"No, I don't suppose I do, but I remember my *own*. Like that, is she?"

"Like that," Nora returned solemnly. "Lift that bar, tote that barr'l. Little girls should be seen and not heard. Like that. You'd better hurry. The colonel won't want to be kept waiting."

"It's only an honorary title," Katie called over her shoulder as she left the kitchen, and so missed the look of relief that swept over the girl's square little face.

"Ah, Katie." The colonel had been poking around the almost-empty room, fingering her mother's collectibles on the shelf beside the fireplace. He was a tiny martinet of a man, barely five feet four, with a moustache out of proportion to his face, and hardly a hair on the top of his head. "I remember your mother kept this room full of furniture."

"Yes, well, times have changed," Katie responded. "Have a chair, Colonel. And some refreshment. Tea?"

"Brandy would be better," he replied. He inspected the dusty couch, and decided to stand. Katie went to the sideboard for a drink, and brought it to him. Colonel Fessenden. He and his family had moved into the district some few years earlier. What he did for a living was still obscure. What his wife did was try to take over the social leadership of the community.

"I'm sorry I missed you at our party," he drawled. He sipped at the brandy in one hand while the other brushed a minuscule speck of dust from the lapel of his sport coat. "You seemed to disappear."

"Your dogs tried to eat me," she said. "I began to feel I wasn't welcome. Did you want something specific, Colonel?" He hadn't earned the title, and she hated to use it on him, but why fight city hall? There were still two or three *real* colonels in the district, with records that demanded respect.

"Not really." Fessenden possessed a very deep voice for such a little man. "I was passing, and remembered I had a small duty to perform."

"Duty?" Katie was puzzled by the phrase. Before her father's death the colonel had shown a great deal of respect for her; not since. What duty could he have toward her?

"Er—yes. Duty," he repeated as he finished off the brandy. "I understand you are forced to sell your farm, Katie. That's a terrible thing, but it happens to us all now and again."

"Does it?" she responded bleakly. His sharp little nose flashed around in her direction.

"And so I wanted you to know I would be happy to buy it from you, my dear. Take the load off your back, so to speak." He reached into his pocket for a calling card, on the back of which he penciled in some figures. "At about that level, should you be interested."

Katie took a quick look. The house alone was worth as much as the colonel was offering for both house and farm. She managed to get her face under command. Her "poker face," her father always called it. And it's too bad that Dad didn't have a poker face, she thought as she tapped the card against her fingernail. I wish I knew with whom he gambled.

"I'll consider it," she told the colonel. "I—have to contact my advisers, you know. I don't know a great deal about land prices."

"Advisers?" The colonel's ears perked up. "You have advisers?"

"Oh, yes," she told him. "I'll let you know, Colonel. And I do thank you for your offer." She was walking toward the front door, and her visitor had no option but to follow. As she closed the front screen door behind him, he turned back to her.

"Don't be too long about it," he said. "Prices change quickly in the real estate business, and I'd hate to have your property go to public auction."

"I understand," she said. "And thank you again." The little man stumped down the steps and headed for his Cadillac, leaving Katie at the door, still tapping her fingernail with the card. And why would he want to buy my farm? she asked herself as she watched. He doesn't farm. He has enough land for his—mansion. Why would he think his price might be acceptable? Is he trying to buffalo me? And just how do you suppose he knew that I had to sell? And why am I so darned suspicious of everyone and everything? She was still pondering the question when she went back to the kitchen.

They were all tired that night. Nora went to bed early, without protest. The Tale of the Four Bears had now progressed to another crisis, and the little girl fell asleep with a smile on her face. "Good story," Jack whispered as he came in for the tail end of the tale. "Can't wait to hear the ending myself. Who wrote it?"

"Shakespeare," she giggled, leading him by the hand out of the room and down the stairs.

"Shall we *set* a spell on the porch?"

"You really *are* a Yankee, aren't you?" she challenged. "People around here don't talk like that at all."

"You bet," he chuckled. "I come from the north. North Croatia, that's my family background."

He seemed to do it without thinking, dropping his arms around her shoulders as they went outside and sank down on the top step. Twilight was on them, and Kate shivered. Not from the cool wind; her sweater took care of that. It was his arm, resting solidly as if it owned the place. And his hand, casually toying with the ends of her hair, with the lobe of her ear as he talked.

He was talking about Tennessee, where he had traveled often, but the words passed right over her head. She was busy forming fantasy, filling her mind with a million miles of him, from the tiny inch he was offering. When he pulled her back against his chest she went willingly, and her contented sigh gave the whole show away. She dreamed until the first stars came out, and would have continued, but his arm had dropped lower, around her waist, and those wandering fingers were playing strange tricks with her mind. She snapped back to attention, moving uneasily as his hand wandered up to her breast. The movement stopped, but the hand remained in place.

"What?" he asked softly.

"I—we won't be able to do this much after the next two weeks," she stuttered. "Mosquitoes, and things that squeak in the night."

"That's not the problem," he said, squelching her movement as well as her speech. He spoke softly, but there was iron in his tone as well as his arm.

"I—I don't know what you mean," she sighed. He laughed and turned her around to face him.

"This is the problem," he answered. He pulled her slowly up against his hard frame, giving her plenty of opportunity to object. The idea never crossed her mind— at that moment, that was. When he offered his lips, brooding over her in the darkness, she made the very tiniest of objections, and then hauled down her flag. It was a repetition of the last time he had kissed her, but this time there was more comfort than passion. When he broke away she whimpered in protest, and pulled his head down again to taste of the wild honey.

Jack laughed, a triumphant male laugh, and bent to her. This time the warmth was swallowed by fire, the comfort by wild passion as he probed her sensitive mouth with his tongue, stroked her back with one hand, and tangled his other in the depths of her hair. When he broke off this time it was only to stand up, sweep her up in his arms, and start for the door.

Her breath and her conscience caught up to her at the same time, just as he fumbled to open the screen door. "What—where are we going?" she gasped.

"Upstairs," he chuckled. "I'm too old for sparking on the front stairs when there are plenty of comfortable beds to be had."

She put out her hand and snatched at the latch. He came to a sudden stop. "What's the matter?" he asked.

"I—I'm too young for playing games in your bed," she said. The words came out in all their bitterness. She didn't *want* to say them. She wanted so very much for him to sweep her up the stairs without a single word being said, and accepting what was bound to come after. But having verbalized it, he had made it cheap. The kind of thing that high-school girls did behind the barn. It was too much for a girl with her narrow upbringing. Too much the sort of thing she could expect from men like Peter.

"Come off it," he snorted.

"Put me down," she snapped. "I may be your landlady, but I'm not your resident——"

"Good God!" he interrupted as he set her feet gently down on the floor of the porch. "You've never done this sort of thing before?" He did not sound bitter. Disappointed—certainly regretful, but not bitter. She backed away from him, trying to hide her face—her too easily read face.

"Is that what you really mean, Katie?"

"What would your wife say?" she countered, fumbling the words over her tongue. She regretted it as soon as it was said, but regrets were possible; recall was not. In the darkness it was impossible to see his reaction, but her fingers told her that his face had turned to stone.

He stood for a moment, then turned on his heel and went into the house, leaving her standing there alone.

Katie turned back to the rail, took three steadying breaths, and glared unseeing out into the distance. The smell of pine filled her nostrils. In the distance, up in the National Park, the lonely sound of a loon echoed in the air. Feeling just as lonely as the bird, she clutched at the rail and let her foolish tears run again. It was a full hour later before she was able to pull herself together and go up to her own bed.

CHAPTER SIX

AN HOUR after Jack left Katie managed to stumble up the stairs into her own bedroom. She bypassed her bath, dropping her clothes as they came off, in little piles on the floor. Neglecting even her nightgown, she dived under the covers, huddled up in a little ball, and cried. The pillows bore mute evidence of the agony. Why? Why? Because he has a wife? She wanted to believe that to be the reason why she'd rejected him. Wanted to, but couldn't. "I don't give a darn about your wife," she whispered into the darkness.

Then why is it? Am I so crazy, so mixed up about my parents? So wanting to be loved—by anyone? Surely not anyone. There had been more than one groping boy in her life. They had all left her feeling just a little bit—dirty. So why now, with *this* man, so suddenly? Just a touch, and she had caught fire. If he had carried her one more step further she would have gone up like a balloon, without hope of salvation. So then it's me, not him. Is that right, girl?

Me. Brought up in the narrowest of ruts—conditioned to act and react, but not to think. When they all preached at me "Bad girls do it, nice girls don't" it had all been a rote reaction. Of *course* that was the right way to act. "Nice girls don't." And I laughed because it was so easy not to. I never did realise how terribly hard it could be, until tonight, to continue to be a "nice girl." I'm beginning to hate the sound of the words. There I was, until today, saving myself—for what? A

twenty-five-year-old virgin, and as proud of my stupidity as any fool could be. Can love be that proud?
And on that note, by light of earliest dawn, Kate finally
fell into an exhausted sleep.

The next three nights were almost frigid. Inside the
house, not outside. The state of Virginia hurried toward
summer. In fact it provided a magnificent pyrotechnic
display, the first major thunderstorm of the year. But
inside the house it might as well have been January. Katie
found herself tiptoeing around the house, doing her best
to avoid Jack, at the same time sharing a growing
relationship with Nora.

"Dad blew it, huh?" the little girl exclaimed one day,
as they worked in the kitchen on a shepherd's pie.

"I don't know what you mean. Make sure there's
plenty of flour on the board before you try to roll the
crust."

"Grandma says he's not very patient. It gets him in
a lot of trouble. He's got a short fuse. At least, that's
what Grandma says."

"I'd rather not talk about your father."

"Isn't that something? That's what *he* said this
morning. You two are a funny pair."

"If you mean your father and I, we're—we're not a
pair at all!" And we ought to be! What good does it do
to go to bed alone and cry into your pillow all night? I
was scared, that's all, not stricken by some darn morality.
If he had given me more warning maybe I could have
adjusted. I could have thought up some nice line like
"your bed or mine?" Or something like that. Instead I
jumped like a jackrabbit and kept running! Despite the
preachments, God didn't intend me to be a virgin for
the rest of my life! It's the only game in the world where

you can only get experience by—by experiencing it. That's a stupid way to put it, but there it is.

"Hey!"

Katie finally felt the hand tugging at her skirt, the raised little voice. "I'm sorry, I must have been miles away. What did you say, Nora?"

"I said, shall I put the pies in the oven now?"

"I—let me inspect the top crust. Yes, that looks good."

"And then I said——"

The front door opened, and footsteps echoed. Katie cocked an ear. "Yes? You said?"

"And then I said if you mean to duck out on Dad you'd better start now, but it's already too late, because——" The little girl squealed in excitement, and ran to the opening kitchen door, yelling, "Uncle Vanya!"

Katie waited in the background while the family greetings were exhausted. Uncle Vanya, with Jack Lee hovering in the background. Uncle was the most *ordinary* man Katie had ever seen. About five feet eight, neat brown hair, a sharp nose—only his eyes, dark and gleaming with intelligence, reminded her of Jack. He wore a suit of some neutral color. When she turned to check on the oven it amazed her to discover she couldn't remember what color it was. Uncle Vanya.

When introduced, he displayed a courtly old-world manner, bowing over her hand, smiling up at her. "Yes," he said in a perfectly innocuous American accent. "Just as my sister described."

"Vanya is *my* uncle," Jack explained. "My mother's brother."

She made him welcome. It wasn't hard. Everything pleased him; he was ready to talk about anything in the world, from the price of apples to the Pittsburgh Steelers.

So the atmosphere in the house lightened, and by dinnertime they were all friends again.

"But I never did hear what you do for a living," she asked as they gathered in the living room for coffee.

"Uncle Vanya's the World's Greatest Detective," Nora announced proudly.

"Retired," the man added, and suddenly Katie recognized that his hair was white, not brown, and there were wrinkles on his forehead. When she said so, he laughed.

"The art of being a good detective," he lectured, "is to be so ordinary that people pay you no attention at all. Turn around, please." He waited until her back was to him. "Now," he continued, "describe me, please." And for the life of her she was unable to do so. She turned back again, shrugging her shoulders, laughing.

"As you said, John," the older man said, "she is so lovely when she smiles."

It was pure nerves that made her spill the coffee as she filled Jack's mug. Nora brought a paper towel, and Uncle Vanya changed the subject, but it took Katie more than a minute or two to restore her cool.

"I don't think you can do any detecting in this area," she said after a time. "Stanfield is such a small town. Even an ordinary-looking stranger would still be a stranger!"

"So we practice the art of deception," the old man chuckled. "I have a partner. He sets up in the town now. A big brash redheaded Irishman. He will go everyplace, make all sorts of noises, be so abrasive, you see, as a decoy. And behind his cover I will go softly as a mouse— and things will happen."

"But—I don't know what it is you're detecting."

"You," the old man chuckled. "You are what I am detecting. And now I must be going. I will not come back, you understand, until the case is settled. If by some accident you should meet me in public you must not acknowledge that you know me. Goodnight, beautiful lady. Be good to my useless nephew." This time he went the whole way, bowing and kissing her hand at the door. When he went out it seemed that he took the fresh air with him into the darkness.

Nora was too excited that night to go to bed on time. It took almost an extra hour of storytelling to settle her down. When the child's eyes finally closed, Katie sat by the bed for another five minutes, trying to make up her mind. It was a useless exercise. She had already decided what she wanted to do—and really just needed to acquire the courage to go and do it. On her way to the doing she detoured by her own room, added a touch of lip gloss, a patina of rouge, and just the veriest fragment of mascara. After all, courage came in many kinds of packages, and package decorating was an Old Dominion custom.

Jack was out on the porch, cloaked by night, when she came downstairs. She went silently to his side, dropping down on the top step just a few inches from him. His massive head turned to acknowledge her, and then went back to studying whatever it was that had attracted his attention. She wanted to blurt out what she had to say, but hadn't "the gumption," as they said in those parts. After all, you couldn't—not after three days of cold silence—plumb down beside a man and say... well, you couldn't, that's all there was to that. So she sat and shared his silence.

It might have been fifteen minutes later that he stirred. "Fascinating, those lights on the mountain. They move like fireflies. I thought the mountaintop was deserted."

"Not entirely," she said softly. "It's part of a National Forest. There are those who come and go up there all the time. It's a marvelous view." A pause. "I liked your uncle Vanya very much."

"And he liked you, Katie. But then, you're a hard girl *not* to like. With a little luck, and Vanya's suspicious nose, we'll find some answers to those questions of yours." He stared off into the distance again. A curtain of stars was unveiled as high-altitude winds blew clouds away. The scent of the valley, loaded with apple blossoms and laurel, filled their nostrils. He sighed, a deep, gusty sigh.

"Katie, I'm sorry that——"

"Jack, I'm sorry——"

Their apologies both started at the same moment, and both stopped. He looked at her. She could see his teeth sparkling by starlight as he grinned. "Ladies first."

"No. You."

"Okay. Katie, I wanted you to know I'm sorry about that affair the other night. I had no right to assume what I did, and——"

Her hand on his sleeve stopped him. "I think perhaps you *had* the right," she said glumly. "I—I wouldn't want you to think I was playing games—playing hard to get, Jack. It was just that it so surprised me that I really was flustered. If I had had any idea what I was doing I wouldn't have been so darn—I wouldn't have said anything like what I *did* say. I was *acting* like some—some idiot. Why shouldn't you think that of me?"

"Nonsense." Both those strong hands were on her shoulders again. "Don't you ever say things like that about yourself again." A triple shake left her in no doubt about his anger. "*I* know you aren't, and *you* know you aren't, and that will be the last time I hear that from you!"

There didn't seem to be anything else to say except "yes sir." She tried it out. It earned her another shake.

"I'm not your uncle," he snapped. "Never mind the *sir* business."

"The thought never crossed my mind," she gasped, "that you might be my uncle." My lover, yes, but not my uncle. Never that, Jack Lee!

That was the right answer, apparently. He urged her to lean in his direction, directing gently with one hand. She turned, resting in his lap and the curve of his right arm, looking up at him, wishing. The kiss came slowly. A feather touch, a circular gliding motion, and then a gentle sealing. His left hand stroked her cheek, then trailed down her willing frame to rest in the little hollow between waist and hip. Like a huge flywheel building up to speed she could feel passion accelerate. She reached for the open neck of his shirt and buried her hand inside against the smooth rock of his chest. Something in the back of her mind, some guardian, kept whispering "hurry." Her inability to know how or in what direction to do the hurrying infuriated her. She whimpered. He moved his head and stared down at her.

"Wow," Jack said. "The other night—what was it that set you off?"

She struggled to get a grip on her runaway emotions. They were hard to rein in—almost impossible. He waited patiently.

"I don't know how to talk about it," she moaned. "It wasn't just—I wanted—there was your wife to consider!'' She offered it as a diversion, only to have him snap it up angrily.

"Oh, my God!'' His hand came back up to her cheek, then threaded through her hair. She could feel his fingers quiver as they explored the hollow behind her ear. He was thinking of something, and his hands moved without purpose. Then he pulled her up to a sitting position, and gently set her back on the step.

"I don't know where you get your information," he said remotely.

"I—Nora told me."

"I see. Now that's something *I* don't like to talk about," he said. "But I'll tell you anyway. I don't have a wife. Six months after Nora was born Helen packed up, cleaned out both our bank accounts, and deserted us. We haven't seen her since. Two years ago I divorced her. It wasn't a happy time for any of us, and I don't suppose she ran off because I was the perfect husband. But that's the way it is. Does that make you feel better?"

"Oh, yes, yes—very much so. I mean, I'm sorry about you and your wife, but——"

"But there's something else?"

"I—yes. There's something else." She ducked her head away from him, her fists clenched. Only the pain of her own fingernails biting into her palms kept her from screaming everything out into the night.

"What?" He was staring at the side of her head, and used a finger to turn her chin back in his direction. His voice was cold. "Now here's where you tell me that nice girls never have done it with strangers?"

"No!" she screamed at him, unable to contain her frustrations. "Damn you!" She beat on his shoulders with her fists. He stopped the attack by grabbing both her fists in one of his hands.

"So what is it, then?" he asked.

She took a deep sobbing breath. "It's because this nice girl has never done it with anybody at all," she mumbled.

"What!"

"You heard me."

"My God! Whoever would have thought...?" he mused. "All the way up into the Blue Ridge, and I find——"

"I know," she said bitterly. "A twenty-five-year-old virgin. I was always proud of the fact, and now it's become an almost intolerable burden to me."

"That's not what I was going to say," he returned. "You prize yourself too lowly. I was going to say I've come all the way up the Blue Ridge and found honesty and an old-fashioned thing called virtue. And being a typical Washingtonian I don't know what to make out of either one of them!"

"Don't build it up into too big a thing," she sighed, moving that additional inch away. "Things don't seem as black or white as they did yesterday. I'm very mixed up. I don't know what's come over me. I didn't mean to tell you anything like that. I wish you would forget it all."

"Everything?"

"I—yes, everything."

"You're not going to ask me to relieve you of this 'intolerable burden'?"

"No."

"Have I insulted you?"

"No."

"Then come back over here where you belong."

"Yes," she sighed again, and barely nipped off the "sir" that tried to follow. Back in the cradle of his arms she luxuriated in the feel and scent and sound of him, his heart beating steadily in the ear she pressed against his chest, his chin resting among the windblown tendrils of her hair. It *was* where she belonged.

"We have a lot of problems, you and I," he half whispered, his lips moving down close to her ear. "And when we get them resolved, lady, we're going to come back to this 'burden' of yours."

Kate stirred uneasily in his arms, making a vague protest. He subdued her with an ounce of extra pressure. "Please don't talk like that," she moaned. "Am I not going to have anything to say about it?" She waited breathlessly for his answer.

"Not much," was the laconic reply. "I'm what you might call the dominating macho man, love."

She shivered at the threat and the promise. Her education almost led her to go into battle over the subject again; her inherited instincts cut off both the words and the thought. She huddled closer, not willing to be separated from him. "And what do we do until then?"

"And until then," he laughed, "we're going to live dangerously." His roaming hands gave description to what he meant.

It rained all that night, and was still drizzling the next morning. The two Lee faces at her breakfast table were glum, to say the least, although they improved considerably when Katie provided hot blueberry pancakes with maple syrup. Well, *almost* maple syrup. And, after stacking all the dishes in the refurbished dishwasher, Jack gave them both a big smile.

"Time for us to have a council of war," he announced. "Coffee in the library, in ten minutes."

His daughter glared at him. "I s'pose I'm gonna disappear, am I?"

"Not at all," he assured the child. "We're a team, us three. But you can have cocoa instead of coffee." They both turned to look at Katie.

"And I suppose I'm going to make the coffee and wait on you hand and foot?" she inquired, allowing a little sarcasm to creep in.

"No," he returned. "I'll make the coffee."

"He makes terrible coffee," his daughter commented. "Grandmother told me that. It'll poison you."

"Nora!"

"Well, it will," the child insisted. Katie pulled the girl over to her side.

"That bad, huh? Then I suppose I'll have to make it just to stay alive?"

"But you don't have to wait on me hand and foot," Jack interjected. How can he make himself sound so serious when his eyes are laughing? Katie asked herself. "Hand is all right," he continued, "but we don't need foot waiting." And then he cocked his head to one side and offered her the most appealing look she had seen in years.

"All right, all right," she gasped, unable to restrain the laughter. "I know a good con game when I see it. Coffee in the library in ten minutes."

They were both waiting for her some twenty minutes later as she pushed the trolley into the room. "I thought maybe a little more toast—and I found a couple of croissants left over. And Nora will pour."

"Me?" the girl said, just a half second before her father said the same thing.

"You," Katie assured her. "Girls have to learn things like that, and now's a good time to practice." She moved around the heavy table and took a chair across from Jack.

"Have I been missing something?" he mused, as his daughter performed faultlessly.

"No, but Lenora might have," Katie told him softly. "She's growing fast. She needs——"

"I need a mother," the child interrupted. "And the sooner the better!"

A quick, deep silence. And then, "Well, I do," Nora repeated. "You've always told me to speak up about 'portant things!"

Katie ducked her head to hide the blush that crowded into her cheeks. Jack Lee seemed to have been overcome by something which choked him. He took a sip at his coffee mug to clear his throat.

"Now, to business," he finally said as his daughter glared at him.

"Daddy——?"

"We'll talk about that together some other time," he offered blandly. "Right now we have to take care of Katie's problem. One problem at a time, that's my motto."

"Never do today what you can put off until to-morrow. That's your motto," his daughter grumbled as she slid back in her chair and folded her arms. Good Lord, Katie thought. Was I ever so smart when I was her age? This girl thinks like a twenty-year old. I'd love to say something about the matter under dispute, but I just don't dare!

Jack Lee rapped on the table a couple of times with the top of his ballpoint pen. "Item," he said, making a note on the big yellow pad in front of him. "During the last year things have changed immensely for the Lovewell family, right?''

Katie nodded. Nora glared.

"For example, your father took up gambling."

"I wouldn't say it quite that way," Katie interjected. "He was always a gambler, but never as bad as——"

"Yes." He made another note. "You have to gamble someplace, with someone. In a small town like this, where? With whom?"

"I don't know," Katie admitted. "He just went—out. As far as I know there aren't any gambling casinos in the valley."

Jack tapped his pen a couple of times, his lips pursed. "Most gambling is cash only," he said thoughtfully. "But, if he was gambling to excess, there might be a time when he needed checks, or credit cards, or—you wouldn't have your father's checkbook around?"

"In the bottom drawer of that desk," she replied, pointing to the ancient roll-top construction that stood in the corner. "You want me to——"

"Yes, but not just at this second," he told her. And then broke off the puzzled look on his face and smiled at her. It was like the sun coming up all over again. Katie could feel the pleasure spreading through her body.

"So..." he continued, tucking the smile away somewhere out of sight. "Your father begins to gamble heavily. Things go from bad to worse, and we come to the day that we met you at the Fessenden place. Let's go over that part again." He made a couple more check marks on his pad. "You are invited to——"

"Hired to," Katie interrupted. "I wasn't there as a guest."

"Okay, hired to." Another two marks on his pad. "And while you're working up steam somehow or another the guard dogs get loose. How often before has that happened?''

''Never, to my knowledge.'' Katie could feel a tension building up inside her. She plucked ineffectually at a loose thread in her skirt.

''But that happens on the day that idiot Filmore runs by a sheriff's car and gets caught by what is probably the dumbest deputy in the county—in your house.''

''True.''

''We heard the deputy say *he* got in by forcing the door. How do you suppose Filmore got in?''

''I'm afraid he had a key,'' Katie murmured. ''Peter— I gave him a key, and he had twenty-five copies made. Everybody in his crowd had one! I get so mad when I think of it! And why couldn't I think of it before then? I'm probably a great match for that deputy sheriff of yours.''

''He's not mine yet,'' Jack said. ''But he will be. Believe me, he will be. Now, suppose we stop right at that point. And what do we have?''

''I haven't the slightest idea,'' Katie returned. Nora squirmed in her chair and waved her hand for attention. Her father nodded in her direction.

''Somebody's trying to scare Katie off,'' she said.

''Scare Katie?'' He nodded again. ''Possibly. Scare her to what? Run away?''

''She wouldn't do that,'' the child observed.

''I think you're right. Scare her to do what else? Sell the farm?''

''But——'' It was a ridiculous thought, but somehow Katie couldn't get the words to come out. ''Don't be silly,'' she finally managed. Both of them stared at her. ''I was already going to have to sell the farm. It wasn't exactly a secret, you know.''

"But perhaps not just at this moment," Jack suggested.

Katie struggled to her feet. "What are you saying? That there's some secret little conspiracy going on? That the town is plotting to get rid of me?"

"Not exactly the town," he told her. "That's what we'll have to find out. Did those dogs get loose by accident? Did this Filmore kid just 'happen' to be speeding by your house? Was the marijuana just a coincidence? Now there are a few questions to start off with. And our time limit is—is what, Katie?"

"Three weeks," she murmured. "That's when I *have* to have the money to settle the estate." She paced the room a couple of times. "I think this whole thing is rubbish. My family have lived in this town for centuries."

"But not everyone in town can say the same," he cautioned her. "But that's enough talking for the moment. Right now I'm due in court."

"In court, Daddy? Is this when somebody's gonna get a zinger?"

"Several somebodies," Jack returned, and that smile was back. "Katie Lovewell strikes back!"

"She does?" A trembling in her legs forced Katie to reach for support. Jack Lee was the only thing available. She grabbed on to him as if her life depended on it.

"She does," Jack said, chuckling. "The kindergarten where you worked is a private outfit, and a knockover. We're filing civil suit against them this afternoon. I think they'll run for cover the minute they hear."

"On what grounds?" Katie asked.

"Oh, I'll think of that on the way to the courthouse," he said. "Civil rights? Anti-feminism? Defamation of character? No, we can't use that one. That's the one you're suing the sheriff on."

"I am?"

"You am. Give us a kiss, ducks. I need a little courage. You're also seeking an injunction against the library for discrimination. Those librarians are hard to handle."

Katie was so completely bedazzled that it hardly seemed worth the bother of trying to avoid his kiss, even though his daughter was standing there, admiring. He enveloped her like her own individual cyclone, whirling her up into the clouds, thoroughly disconcerting her mind, and then dropping her and rushing for the door.

Katie turned slowly and stared at Nora. "Your father," she said solemnly through dry, trembling lips, "is a man of violent passions."

"I ain't sure what that means." The girl reflected for a moment. "If you mean he's a sort of wild one, yeah! That's what Grandma always keeps saying. You know, most of the other women he kisses sort of hang on and come up laughing. Maybe you take the whole thing too seriously. Do you think?"

And that's the prize thought, Katie Lovewell thought. I'm taking instruction from a nine-year old child on how to kiss her father! And maybe it's not a bad idea. I'm not doing too well all by myself, am I? But there was an afterthought, one that had a tinge of bitterness to it. "You mean he kisses a lot of women?"

"I couldn't count high enough," Nora responded. "I'm only in the fourth grade, you know."

CHAPTER SEVEN

KATHLEEN rode her bicycle into town the next morning. There was a horde of little things to be done among the few stores in Stanfield, and Jack had gone off with his daughter in tow. An old-fashioned town, Stanfield, like any of the ten thousand you might see throughout the rural south. Main Street went north and south, forming the western border of Court House Square. The white-pillared Baptist church occupied one corner. The Episcopal church sat on the opposite side of the diamond in all dignity. The Methodist church sat back from the street demurely, surrounded by its own grove of oaks. And the courthouse commanded all of the north side. A stately row of maple trees surrounded and sheltered the square. At least half the trees had been there to see General Jackson as he had driven his foot cavalry up the valley during the War Between the States.

As Katie came out of the pharmacy with a handful of parcels she ran into Evvie Hamilton, the man who controlled the dogs on the Fessenden estate. It was too good an opportunity to miss. "Day off, Evvie?"

"Half day," he drawled. "Miz Fessenden don't go much for full days off. Ain't seen you around much, lately."

"Busy," she admitted. "Care to take a cup of coffee with me?"

"Don't mind if I do," he agreed, and led her down the block to the Stanfield Coffee Shoppe. They found an empty table in the corner, and ordered.

119

"Miss your dad, I do." Evvie sipped at his mug. He was a man who would never see sixty again, with a fringe of white hair, and one missing tooth right in the middle of his weather-beaten grin.

"I do myself," she answered. "But we have to get on with living, don't we? How are the dogs?"

"Funny. You're the third one to ask me that in the last three days." He managed another sip. "You'd think it was a big thing, that with the dogs. The sheriff's deputy asked me that very question. Well, no, that ain't right. He *told* me that the gate lock must of been broke."

"The deputy?"

"Strange, ain't it? Him and Miz Fessenden, they makin' out like a pair of bandits when the colonel's not around. Can't quite imagine that. She's hunting high society, and he's lower than a raccoon's belly, but well, it ain't my business to talk."

"So that was it," Katie murmured. "The lock was broken."

"Well, now, I didn't rightly say that, Miss Katie. The *deputy* said the lock was broke. I looked at it that same day. Wasn't nothin' wrong with the lock, 'cept somebody unlocked it. Miz Fessenden gave me a line of chatter about broken locks the next day, so I went back to check. And what do you know?" He grinned at her across the table. "There was a new lock on the gate, and the old one done completely disappeared! Now how's that for a mystery?"

"It surely is something," she agreed, but was hard put to keep her mind on the conversation. Someone had unlocked the gate. Why? Who? Katie was unable to sit still. She just *had* to move. Making a quick excuse, she left the shop and went out into the sunshine. One of the old men playing checkers across the square waved to her.

She waved back, and stepped out into the street. As she remembered it later the first sound was that of a motor accelerating. The screech of brakes came later, almost too late. She barely turned her head in the direction of the noise before the heavy truck skidded. The left front corner of the bumper caught her in the thigh as she tried to move out of the way, and tossed her back onto the pavement, where she collected a crowd in a hurry.

"Are you hurt, Katie?" She managed to focus on the face leaning over her. It was the driver of the truck, Peter Lester. With her vision blurred it was hard to see the expression on his face.

"Only my pride," she muttered as she managed to sit up.

"You walked right out in front of me," Lester insisted. "You all saw, didn't you?"

A couple of younger men in the crowd made agreeing noises, but there was a background argument. "Didn't see you really try to stop," Evvie Hamilton said.

"You want to watch what you say, old man," Lester warned. "You've got no call going around making accusations. Accidents happen. Sometimes they're God's warning."

There was a bustle at the edge of the crowd, and Jack Lee appeared at Katie's side. He dropped to one knee to examine her. He was all business, running his hands over her legs, checking the bruises on the side of her head. "Nothing terribly bad," he murmured as he supported her back. "But we'll get you to the hospital just the same. One of you people call the ambulance."

Katie's head was whirling. The bruises hurt, but still everything seemed to be so funny, sounded so hollow. Except for Jack. She leaned back into the warm comfort of him and giggled. "We don't have an ambulance."

"All right, love," he comforted her. "That's a little concussion you've got there, I'll bet. I'll drive you to the hospital."

"And we don't have one of those, either," she sighed. "You have to go over to Front Royal to find a hospital. Or down to Dr. Franklin's clinic at Luray."

"Oh, brother!" she heard him mutter, but the words were indistinct. And in a moment Nora was with him. "Hold on to her while I get the car," he told the girl. Katie felt the change of arms as the child settled down beside her. There were other hands to help; Katie felt the need to keep her eyes closed. But she heard everything that was said.

"Run over my girl, did you?" Jack Lee, talking to somebody. *At* somebody, for a fact. Katie, who hated violence, shuddered and shut her eyes.

"It was an accident," Peter Lester blustered. There was a tremor of fear in his voice, which made Katie feel ever so much better. "Anybody can tell you it was an accident."

"Accidents don't happen to *my* girl." There was a satisfying thud and a gasp from the crowd. Katie decided to make the sacrifice, and opened one eye. Peter Lester was sitting in the middle of the pavement. There was something wrong with his very handsome nose. Jack Lee leaned over and pulled him back up to his feet, then casually brushed him down and straightened the younger man's shirt collar.

"Accidents *never* happen to my girl," Jack said in a low, warning voice. "Got that? *Never* happen to my girl."

"I—I've got it," Peter said.

"Good. I like a quick learner." With which Jack gave him a little push, and Peter was back sitting on the curb again with blood running out from between his fingers.

"I'll get the car," Jack continued in a casual voice. "You folks watch over my girl?"

"I don't know what you're making such a big fuss about," Katie grumbled. The trip to the clinic had exhausted the rest of the day, and all that Dr. Franklin had had to say was, "Go home, keep off your feet, take two of these, and call me in the morning."

"Even the doctor said it was only a little bruising," Katie complained. "*I'm* the one who got hit, and you're going around with a sore head, like some bear caught at the beehive! Why in the world would Peter Lester want to run me down? Everything you turn to seems to be some deep conspiracy. For God's sake, it was only a trivial accident. I didn't look where I was walking."

"He also said it might be a concussion," he muttered as he stamped back and forth in the living room. And wearing my carpet to the nub, she thought as she watched his feet, not daring to watch his face. The whole idea seemed worth a giggle. She tried it out tentatively as she shifted her weight on the couch.

"It's not funny," he snapped as he whirled around and stomped over directly in front of her. She looked up at the furious face he wore, and then that crumpled, he dropped to his knees, and gathered her up as gently as if she were a Ming vase. "My girl doesn't have accidents," he muttered in her ear. "Damn you. You've got to be more careful, woman!"

"Everybody has accidents," she murmured. One of those huge hands of his stroked through her hair. Well, it's one way of getting attention around here, she told herself, and again the giggle escaped.

He set her back into the depths of the couch, and carefully rearranged the pillows behind her. She relaxed against them with a sigh of relief. It *had* been a strenuous day. Jack Lee settled back on his haunches. Even in that position he was nose to nose with her. Nora came in from the kitchen, carrying a glass beaded with frost.

"Lemonade," the girl offered as she handed over the glass, and then took a quick look at her father. "Lecture time," she giggled, and made for the door before his glare caught up with her.

"The voice of experience?" Katie held the glass to her lips, not to sip, but to have something between herself and this—man.

"You'd better believe it," he muttered. "That's all I need. Another female as sharp-tongued as my daughter. Why me, Lord?"

"I don't know," she mused. "Been to church lately?"

"And that," he growled as he rose to his full length, "will be enough of that. Listen up, lady."

I should stand and bow, Katie told herself. And probably kiss his foot. But being the patient gave her *some* rights, so she merely nodded. He began his little speech; she heard not a word. There was something attractive about how his chin bobbed as he emphasized his words. How his eyes gleamed darkly, how the tip of his right ear seemed to wiggle on occasion. How that black curl fell down across his forehead when he gestured—and he did a great deal of that. A woman, she told herself, would find it terribly difficult not to succumb to his blatant masculinity. Aren't I? And then the silence rang in her ears. She brought herself back to reality, startled by the quiet.

"Well?" Hands on hips, legs slightly apart, he towered over her the way the Colossus might have towered over the harbor at Rhodes, controlling her every entry point, every thought. And she had no idea which sheet of music he was singing from.

"Perhaps," she muttered.

He exploded. "Perhaps! What the devil does *that* mean, woman?"

"Perhaps you'd better repeat a little of that," she sighed. "Like everything after 'Listen up.'"

For a moment he looked as if he might be ready to explode. Katie shivered and pulled back to the depths of the sofa. And even as she moved his red face smoothed, his eyes shifted from storm to twinkle, and the corners of his mouth turned up. When he laughed it was with raucous enthusiasm, with what her father used to describe as a two-county laugh.

"Didn't hear a word, huh?"

"I—was busy thinking," she admitted, and then ducked her head. "Did I miss a lot?"

"Not really," he returned. "Katie Lovewell, I've been looking for a woman like you for years!"

"Well, I've been right here all the time," she told him wistfully. There was a touch of sadness in the words, too. She wished he had looked *faster*, or come sooner. She had wasted so much time looking around among unsatisfactory men! And he had had the colossal nerve to marry another woman! But then if he hadn't there wouldn't be Nora, would there? And she loved the practical little girl almost as much as she loved her father. So, filled with vague pains and strong pleasures, she said nothing. Even when he leaned over and added a massive hug to all her problems. And barely an hour later, prohibiting any further interesting developments, Uncle Vanya arrived.

"You couldn't find a better Croation meal this side of the ocean," the old man said some time later as he carefully wiped his moustache and set his spoon down. "Your mother teaches you to do this, John?"

"Me," Nora interjected. "Grandmother taught *me*. Papa can hardly boil water, and Katie is too tender to cook."

"Too tender don't need cooking," the old man chuckled. "But I hear about the accident, lovely lady."

"Accident, hell!" Jack commented. They all turned to stare at him.

"Ah, you may be right." Uncle Vanya nodded his head in agreement.

"Right there on the square in broad daylight?" Katie shook her head doggedly. "Not possible. And Peter Lester, for heaven's sake? Why in the world would Peter do something like that?"

"For the normal reasons," the old man said slowly. "For vengeance, for profit. One or the other, or maybe both?"

"You can cross out vengeance," Katie retorted. "He was never in love with me. There'd be no reason for vengeance. And I don't have anything that he could profit from. Look around you. Does this old house indicate a profit motive?"

"As it stands, no," Jack said. There seemed to be signals flashing across the table from him to his uncle, signals that they both understood. "And maybe it isn't the house, but the land it stands on."

"Hah!" She shook her head at their ignorance. "I can't even give it away. Are you suggesting there's oil on the land, or something?"

"Nora," Jack said. "Why don't you clear the table while your Uncle and I have a talk with Katie—in the living room."

The little girl turned to Katie and shrugged her shoulders. "See what I mean? Little pitchers, and all like that. I suppose I have to wash the dishes, too?"

"I'll come and help after a while," Jack promised. "Now then, Miss Lovewell—isn't that a grand name, Uncle Vanya? Come on, now." And before she could catch her breath Katie was up in the air again, swung up in his arms as if she were a five-pound sack of flour rather than a hundred and forty pounds of full-grown woman, and headed for the living room. If it were not for the pain in her thigh she might have enjoyed the whole thing. Especially where the weight of her rested on his right arm, which came around her back and anchored a hand barely an inch below the swell of her attentive breast. But how could you tell a man you hardly knew, whose daughter was staring after them, that she wouldn't object if he got a better handhold?

So when he carefully folded her onto the living-room sofa and reworked the pillows to her satisfaction she was almost purring. And when Uncle Vanya made the coffee and brought it out she had almost forgotten her pains and aches, and *was* purring like a contented cat. And then Jack poured cold water all over her parade.

"You've heard of the East Coast Megalopolis?" he casually inquired. Katie fumbled for a moment. Not because she didn't know, but rather because her mind was deep-diving on another track entirely.

"You mean that prediction that because the cities are expanding so rapidly that pretty soon there'll be just one metropolis, stretching from Boston to Washington? But that's a twenty-first century concern."

"All the way to Richmond, Virginia," he corrected. "And it's already started to happen. Some of the largest construction companies in Washington are looking farther afield right now, trying to find a nice sizable tract worth developing for luxury housing. The only thing that limits their search is access."

"I can see that, but what does it have to do with me?"

"As the crow flies from Washington, Miss Lovewell," he announced pompously, "where is there a nice undeveloped valley area with plenty of land available, good water, lovely view, moderate climate?"

"Am I supposed to guess?" she asked weakly.

"And if you substitute helicopter service instead of the crow flying?"

"You don't mean—here? In our valley? Along the South Fork?"

"Here," he said amiably. "In your valley. And only a half hour from Washington by helicopter. Along the South Fork of the Shenandoah."

"Well, I'll be tongue-tied and dipped in goose grease!" she muttered. "Here?"

"Here. To be exact, *right* here, lovely lady," Uncle Vanya interrupted. "This farm, this house, this land. The planning has been going on for months, and the word evidently has leaked out. In fact, the major consortium was planning to bid on the land in about thirty days."

Jack came over to the couch and perched on its arm, one warm hand ruffling her hair. "And so you see," he said in a soft, solemn voice, "why there are a select few in the valley hoping to acquire the Lovewell farm very quickly?"

"B-but——" she stuttered.

"And why," Uncle Vanya added, "that same select group would like to scare you off, get you to move?"

"Quickly," Jack chimed in. They both stared at her, waiting for an answer which did not come. Jack's hand continued its warm seeking within the massive fold of her hair, mesmerizing her.

"Katie?"

"I don't understand, really," she said. "There's one group in Washington that wants to build in this area? Then why would someone in the valley want me to move out?"

"Because——" and now his voice was harsh "—the local sharks haven't the skill or the capital to develop the area themselves, but if they can get their hands on title to the land they can hold up the people in Washington, and make a killing. And all they have to do is get Miss Katie Lovewell to sell out to them. How's that for a profit motive?"

She shook her head at him. "Not my friends," she murmured. "My family has lived here forever. Nobody would do anything like that for——"

"They're not *all* your friends. Come on, Katie, don't walk around with blinkers on. Has anyone offered for the land?"

"My lawyers," she offered. "They—really didn't want the land, they just wanted to help me pay off my dad's debts."

"Sure they did." Both men grinned at her. Almost like a pair of sharks, she told herself, but then they're the good guys. Aren't they?

"And then there was Colonel Fessenden," she added.

"And what do we know about the good colonel?" Uncle Vanya asked.

"He owns a nice estate, but not enough land for a major development," Jack retorted.

"And those dogs of his didn't get loose by accident," Katie said apologetically. "Somebody tampered with the lock on their kennel run."

Both men looked at her, startled. "Tampered with the lock?"

"Well, Evvie said the lock had been——" her voice fell an octave, as she almost whispered "—unlocked."

Jack Lee muttered something in Croatian, and smashed one of his fists into his other palm. Uncle Vanya made soothing noises. Nora poked her head around the kitchen door to listen, and then suddenly disappeared.

"What is it?" Katie stared at both men, and at Nora's disappearing back. "I——"

"My nephew," Uncle Vanya said. "He lives like the—firecracker? That is the word? Any little problem and he blows the head off? My apologies. It is hard to believe he is the lawyer in the family, no?"

"I believe," Katie said quickly. "Anything he says, I believe."

Uncle Vanya struck his forehead with an open palm. "Quick," he admonished his nephew. "Take the lady. Go north to Front Royal, where is a good church, and marry her before she recovers. Or maybe go south instead. In Staunton they got such a grand mental clinic!"

And by that time Jack had recovered his aplomb. "The name of the game is conspiracy," he said. "Katie becomes the target suddenly, the day of her piano recital at the Fessendens'. Some amateur cop tries to involve her in a drug episode. Then someone sets the dogs loose. The next day she goes into court——"

"And if you hadn't appeared they would have chopped me up into hamburger," she interrupted. Jack nodded and smiled at her. A brief smile. It flashed in her direction like a lighthouse beam, and then was gone.

If Katie had been more mobile she might have changed course toward that lighthouse, but her muscles were too bruised, her head ached, and the telephone rang. And a moment later Nora came into the room.

"What?" Jack asked. Nora shrugged her shoulders.

"A man called, on the telephone," she said.

"What man?"

"He didn't say," the little girl responded. "He just said to tell Vanya that it's going down the day after tomorrow."

"And that's all?"

"That's all we need," Uncle Vanya said. "We have to go, John. Right now. We've got a lot of things to get done before dawn."

"But hell, I can't leave Kathleen alone here! Who knows what'll happen?"

"Who knows what won't happen?" Vanya snapped. "There is Lenora. She could stay?"

"Not good enough," Jack returned. "Not good enough. By Satan and all his devils, why now? We need another——" He stopped in midsentence and stared at his uncle. They both ruminated and then looked at Nora.

The little girl's smile collapsed. "Oh, no," she said, sighing.

"Oh, yes," her father said. At which all three of the Lees stepped into the adjoining room, leaving Kate all alone among her daydreams.

It was more than an hour later when a solemn little Nora came back to the living room, and coughed. Katie, who had been up to her ears in dreams about apple blossoms and organ music, came to with a start. "Nora? Where's your father?"

"They're both gone," the little girl reported. Something was bothering the child. She was standing in front of the couch, using the toe of one shoe to scratch the back of the other leg, and occasionally swiping at her eyes with a dry knuckle. "They left about an hour ago. Dad said—not to worry, that he'd be back for sure. Uncle Vanya didn't say nothin'."

"Well, isn't that curious?" Kate was still struggling out of the fog of her dream.

"Men!" Nora stabbed at her eyes again. "It ain't curious, it's downright aggravatin'. But I suppose all men are like that?" She looked up at Kate, who had managed to struggle to her feet.

And how in the world would I know about "all men"? Kate asked herself. Those lovely eyes were glued to her, and an answer must be provided. Kate took a deep breath, and crossed the fingers on her right hand, behind her back. "Yes, it's the sort of thing most men might do," she said. "There's no need for us to worry? Who the devil does your father think he is, telling us not to worry. We'll worry or not as we wish, that's what we'll do. Men don't own the world, even though they think they do! They've made a terrible mess about everything. It's time we women took over the reins!"

"That's great," Nora said gleefully. "That man needs somebody to set him down now and again——" And then, somewhat more subdued, "Only I ain't got the nerve. You're gonna do wonders for this family."

Yes, I certainly am, Kate thought. If only I get an invitation to join, and if Jack and I learn how to get along with each other, and if—— What about Grandmother, who, according to Nora, rules the roost? "I'm not sure I have the nerve, either, Nora. But with the two of us together I think we could handle things.

And now, little bit, don't you think it's time for both of us to get to bed?"

The night seemed to have thirty-six hours. Nora, whose room was separated from Kate's by a shared bath, pleaded to have the connecting doors open. Kate sat by the little girl's bed, pushing her fantasy tale of the Four Bears to its furthest point. Nora tossed and turned and finally crossed over into dreamland at about ten o'clock.

Kate went off to bed herself, after a careful quiet shower. As she patted herself dry she looked over her shoulder into the huge mirror opposite the tub. No doubt about it, she told herself grimly, if life continues on like this I'm going to be black and blue and yellow for the rest of my life. She powdered those places she could reach, and went gingerly to bed herself.

It was not exactly a toss-and-turn night. It was more like a toss-and-squirm night. Every time she tried to turn over her scratches and bruises reminded her of reality. And every time she managed to drop off she was dominated by a strange nightmare, the one where she was being chased by the two slavering dogs who were getting close enough to bite. And then Jack appeared out of the darkness, the dogs stopped while he patted them and gave them a cheerful "well done, boys," and then he commanded the dogs to continue their attack. Over the dogs' muzzles Jack's face seemed to expand and his perfect white teeth turned into yellow fangs, moving closer and closer—and then Kate woke up, shivering and perspiring in the cool breeze coming in through her open window.

At about three in the morning Kate had had enough. She slid carefully out of bed, and went downstairs. The house was old; it creaked in the night winds. Kate had known this for years. Nevertheless, coming downstairs now, with all her thoughts scrambling themselves, she jumped at every squeak, winced at every slam or bang as the wind wrestled in the shingles. By the time she had finished warming a mug of chocolate she was a nervous wreck.

She warmed her hands on the outside of the mug, picked up a blanket from the sofa, and then hobbled outside to the steps, where she huddled up against the stair post and peered out into the shadows. Shadows because the moon had sprinkled the area with a tiny bit of light, and the sweet smell of lilacs floated on the breeze. She set the mug aside for a moment, and wrapped herself up in the light blanket. It provided just enough warmth to make her comfortable. She picked up the mug again, nursed on the warm, sweet drink, and dreamed.

Jack Lee. What a strange and complicated man. He could fix "everything" with his hands and almost anything else with his mind. He was not, perhaps, the most handsome man in the world, being just a little too imperious for all of that. He had a beautiful daughter. And a line of blarney that would astonish the Sphinx. And I love him very much! Kate grinned at that last statement. It was all true, and she might as well admit it, for all the good that it did. She wrapped her hands around her knees and rocked back and forth for a moment. The morning star was rising at just that moment. It stood like a beacon, almost alone in the dawn sky. But I was never Nefertiti, she told herself, and the thought saddened her.

"Couldn't sleep neither?" A soft, lovely voice. Katie turned her head slightly. There were two bare feet balancing themselves on the top stair beside her. Nora, in her cotton granny nightgown, white with red rosebuds scattered from its high neck to its low hem. The little girl looked pale in the breaking dawn, as if she knew something that frightened her.

"Set a spell?" Kate patted the stairs beside her. Nora sank down, and Katie shared the blanket with her as the pair of them huddled side by side.

"You *do* love my dad?"

"Hard to believe, but I do. Honest Injun."

"Me too." A moment of silence. "I'm scared. There's somethin' mean goin' on in this town."

"But what?" Kate shifted slightly so that she could keep the girl in her direct line of sight.

"I don't know *what*. I just know *is*! That don't make much sense, does it?"

"Doesn't," Kate corrected automatically. "That *doesn't* make sense." Another pause while the pair of them reflected. "On the other hand——" Kate looked down at the beautiful head of hair beside her as she unwound one arm from under the blanket and wrapped it around Nora. "On the other hand, it *does* make sense, if you follow me."

"Yeah." A hand crept into Kate's. "It's too bad. I wish—you'd make one heck of a mother, Katie Lovewell!"

"Oh? I don't get a chance to play in the game? Something your dad said?"

Nora blushed. "I—I just snooped," she said. "He told——"

"He who?"

"Daddy, of course. He told Uncle Vanya that you were too good for the likes of him."

"Ah." Kate shifted again. Her damaged bottom was complaining about sitting still too long on a hard wooden step.

"Well, I don't mean you should quit," Nora protested. "It's worth a chance, ain't it?"

"I'm not likely to quit," Kate said. "I never even got started. I probably am too good for him, but you know, Nora, there are more women than men in this world. It doesn't come out even no matter what we'd like. And that being the case, even though I *am* too good for him, I'm going to get him anyway!"

"Now I'm glad to hear that," Nora said, sighing. She leaned over and rested her entire weight on Kate's shoulder. "I'm in your corner, you know."

Another pair of smiles was exchanged, and then there was silence until the predawn expanded itself into the tiny noises that together heralded the day. Not the roosters; they never seemed to know what time it was. But rather the rustle of bluebirds and robins as they swung out into the country, looking for both the early and the late worm. And the chorus of tree frogs, punctured faintly by the barking of some dog halfway over in the next county. And a low-pitched rumble, far distant in the sky.

"What do you suppose that is?" Nora asked sleepily.

"Airplane," Kate said. "Sometimes they cross the valley, but hardly at *this* hour. Maybe some amateur pilot who's lost his way?"

"Anything could happen," Nora sighed. The pair of them searched the dawn sky as the noise became louder. And louder. And louder.

"What in the world . . . ?" Katie yelled as the blue and white helicopter took a turn around the open garden in front of them, and then came to a halt not more than twenty-five feet from the steps before cutting its motor.

"Oh, my!" Nora gasped. The little girl has better eyes than me, Kate thought as she tried to blink away the dust raised by the whirling blades.

"Oh, my goodness," Nora said. She shook herself out of the blanket and went running down the stairs, barefoot, and dressed only in her nightgown. Kate, who was hardly a bit better off as far as dress was concerned, tightened the blanket around her and wished she was ten miles away. Something even stranger was happening. Nora halted her rush halfway between the stairs and the helicopter as the side door of the machine opened, and the copilot climbed down and turned to assist the passenger to disembark.

And, in the middle of a spring morning in the 1990s, the little girl who was too advanced for her age gathered her nightgown together in both hands and curtsied.

The old woman was dressed in black, except for the string of pearls around her neck. A long black dress that fitted her rotund little form to a nicety, and reached down to within inches of her high-topped boots, with a flash of white lace at the high collar and wrists. Her white hair was arranged in a neat chignon, with not a hair out of place despite the helicopter's wind. Little Nora ran across the space that separated them, and bowed to kiss the extended hand. It was a small enough ceremony. Very impressive, whatever it means, Kate told herself as she gradually rose, doing her best to wrap the blanket more carefully around her. Nora, a few feet away, broke out into a wide smile at something the old woman said, and managed to kiss the cheek proffered before they turned and started the stately march toward the stairs, chattering away.

They came to a halt at the bottom of the stairs. Kate, not knowing what to say, offered something between a half bow and a nod of the head, and then added a somewhat tentative smile.

Nora broke out into a gale of giggles, which lasted just long enough for the lady to nudge her and say reprovingly, "Lenora!" The little girl stifled her laughter, pushed and shoved at her face until it was solemnity itself, and said, "Grandmother, may I present Miss Kathleen Lovewell?" The closely cropped white curls nodded gently. "Katie," the girl continued, "My great-grandmother, Eleana Nostrova Evanov, of the House of Karageorgeovic."

Oh, God, Kate muttered under her breath. What do I do now?

CHAPTER EIGHT

"AND so you see," the little white-haired lady said as she sipped at her cup of tea, "it isn't all that difficult to understand. Pay attention now. We of the elder generations have been so accustomed to all the old-world courtesies. The House of Karageorgeovic has long since been wiped out of existence. Except for me. Most of the royal houses of Europe have also vanished into convents, prisons, poverty. Me, I am different. My grandfather had the foresight to feel the wind of revolution rising, so he packed us all up and brought us to America. Did you know the Karageorgeovic family once ruled the kingdom of Serbia?"

The old lady smiled at Katie's astonished look. "But of course you would not know. Why, even the kingdom of Serbia has disappeared. And that's why I insist that the children of my family practice the amenities—in memoriam, you might say. And you can tell your friends, my dear. It might do something for your reputation to know you are consorting with a former princess. If it hadn't been for the disappearance of the Serbian kingdom, and the willfulness of the House, I—yes, me— would be the pretender to the throne! Are you impressed?" Another gamine grin ran across her unwrinkled face. "Don't be *too* impressed, my dear. As it is, I am just the grandmother of the Lee family. Now, let me see, what should you call me—do you have a grandmother of your own?"

"No," Katie said. "Not a one."

"Then," the matriarch said as she squared her little shoulders and assumed an almost imperial stance, "you shall call me Grandmother also. Is it not so?"

"But I——"

The old lady held up a hand. "No, no, Kathleen. No humble gratitude. My grandson has told me all about you, and all about his plans."

Well, then why the devil didn't he tell *me*? Katie grumbled to herself. Or is this the way one becomes a member of the House of Serbia? By royal fiat? If that— if that man ever shows up again I'm going to show him a few favorite tricks of my Cherokee ancestors—and they certainly have a longer history than Serbia!

"B-but I thought he was Croatian," she managed to stammer.

"Well, to my shame," Grandmother said placidly, "there was none of the Serbian royalty left, and I had celebrated my eighteenth birthday with no one in sight, so I was forced to undertake a marriage somewhat below my station in life—yes, to a Croatian, whose only possession in the world was my deep and abiding love. How I miss that man! And my grandson is a fine example of the result. The blood must be mixed from time to time or it grows thin, no?"

"Now I'm completely lost," Katie admitted. "John is your son?"

"Grandson, my dear."

"And Nora is your——?"

"Granddaughter. Ah, I see. You think a woman of my position wishes to be somebody with a great-granddaughter? And then Nora marries young—it is a trait in my family—and presently I am a great-great-grandmother? Bah! A woman has her pride, is it not so? Grandmother is as far as I go! So they are all my grand—whatever. You must humor an old woman. Would you believe that I am ... seventy-five?''

I would believe, Kate told herself very solemnly, eighty-five. Or even ninety. But she managed a smile, and said, "I find it hard to believe, Grandmother. Have some more cookies?''

"It might not be good for my figure," said the little round creature. But she reached for the plate, and Kate could see that self-same twinkle that starred her grandson's eyes from time to time.

"Kate—I mean Miss Kathleen—is a whale of a good cook," Nora said. "Won't it be great to have someone in the house who knows how to cook?''

"A lovely idea," her grandmother replied, sighing. "You know, little one, when I was your age, before the First World War, we actually had six cooks and one chef in our home. But where the devil is that boy? Kathleen?''

"I'm afraid I don't know." Kate shook her head and ducked away from the matriarch's discerning eye. "Last night—he just went away. He didn't say goodbye, he just went away. And his uncle Vanya with him."

"Ah, Vanya—another rascal, that one. But not even a goodbye at all?''

"Not a word." Kate looked at Nora, hoping for support. The little girl shrugged her shoulders. "Not a word," Kate repeated. "There was a telephone call, and he took a message, and that's all I know." Her head drooped like a tattered flower, and there were almost tears. But I won't cry, she told herself. Not for me, not for him, not for anything!

"Hmmm," the princess pondered. "Vanya was in Washington last night. In fact he brought me word then."

Nora jumped in before Kate could, to her terrible shame, make a fool out of herself over that man. "What was the message?" Nora asked excitedly.

"Why, nothing much, my dear. It was that I was needed urgently in Virginia to—er—baby-sit two little girls, was the way it came out. And so I had the maids pack, and the helicopter ordered up, and here I am."

A helicopter instead of a coach and four, Katie sighed to herself. Even if he asked me, how could I fit into a family like this? As the Irish scrubwoman? And what would they say if they knew I was one quarter Cherokee, from the Western Nation? Where *is* that man?

Nora started to add something to the conversation when the telephone rang. In the two-horse race Nora won, but only because Kate was still hobbling from the damage to her structure. "It's for you," Nora said as she handed over the instrument. The child looked as if someone had stolen her last lollipop.

"It's not my fault." Nora would have nothing of *anyone's* apology. Katie took up the receiver. "Hello?"

"Hello. Miss Lovewell? This is Colonel Fessenden."

I'm going to get rid of this telephone, Kate told herself. The only people who call me are the ones I don't want to have call me! And they all want to tell me something that I don't care to know! "Yes, Colonel?"

"Miss Lovewell—Katie. I find myself running foolish errands for my wife. Is her lawyer there at your house?"

"Her lawyer? I'm afraid I don't know the man, Colonel."

"Oh? I was sure you did. My wife—oh, well, it isn't important. If he should come by, please tell him that the auction will be held tomorrow morning."

"Well, I'd be glad to deliver the message," Kate said quietly, "if only I knew who he was."

"Why, Mr. Lee, of course. I was sure you——"

Whatever else the colonel had to say was never recorded. Katie Lovewell, at the end of her rope, gave a great sigh, dropped the telephone, and slid gracefully down onto the living-room rug in a dead faint.

"Well, it wasn't my fault," Nora muttered for the third time. "Whoever heard of a girl fainting?" Katie opened one eye. She was stretched out on the rug beside the couch with a pillow under her head and a blanket spread neatly over her.

"Why, in my day girls did that all the time," Grandmother contributed. "And Kathleen did it very well. Neatness, you know. One cannot just faint away and fall down. One must be —*chic*?"

"I never fainted in my life," Katie interjected weakly, to no good purpose.

"She did it nicely, I'll give her that," Nora agreed. "I wonder if she could do it better with a little more practice? Are you sure we can't pick her up and put her on the couch?"

"I'm sure," the matriarch said. "You are a very small person, Lenora, and I am too. Besides, a royalty does not become a beast of burden."

"I *never* faint," Kate repeated. "I never——"

"I hear you, child. There's no need to be abusive about it. You never faint. So climb up and lie down on the couch. We both of us couldn't pick you up."

The telephone rang again, just as Kate settled back on the couch. Nora ran for the instrument as Grandmother tucked another pillow behind Kate's back. "It's for Kate again," Nora reported, stretching the flexible cord over to the couch.

"I can get up to do that," Kate said. No matter what Serbian matriarchs did, Virginia women answered the telephone standing up. She staggered to her feet, and then promptly fell over again. "But I'll make an exception for now," she said much more humbly.

"Lie back," Grandmother insisted before she would let Kate hold the telephone. "Put your head a little higher on this pillow. There, that looks rather well. Now go ahead. I'm sure it's good news!"

"Yes, I'm sure it must be." Kate reached for the instrument, almost convinced by the two smiling faces. "Hello," she offered, and listened, then quietly passed the telephone back to Nora, and stared out of the window across those beautiful acres that the Lovewells had owned for almost two hundred years.

"Kate?" Nora shook her shoulder gently. "Katie?"

"Kathleen?" Grandmother Lee knelt by the couch, a worried look on her usually placid and unfurrowed face.

"Katie!" Nora's panic-stricken voice rose a half octave.

Katie Lovewell waved a hand vaguely in their direction. "The sheriff's office," she muttered in a deadly undertone. "I must have gotten the days wrong. They have foreclosed on the farm, and will auction it off tomorrow," Kate sighed, but held back the tears.

Nora groaned a protest as she threw her arms around Kate. "They can't do that," she sobbed. "Can they?"

"You bet your last dinar they can't," Grandmother said firmly.

It was an altogether different group that gathered around the kitchen table after dinner. With just one or two determined words the last representative of the House of Karageorgeovic had changed from a sweet, doddering old lady to a lioness protecting her young. Two long-distance telephone calls had brought help. Four husky young men arrived by helicopter at about six-thirty, each holding the leash on a fit and ferocious Doberman pinscher. Grandmother provided instructions at high speed. All four men grinned, as if they were looking forward to some exercise, and then the house settled down.

"You know," Grandmother said at about eight o'clock, "our family operates a service agency, with our own detectives, lawyers, and so forth."

"And Grandmother is the head of it all," Nora interjected. "Really, Kate, you can't win at stud poker if you smile every time you get an ace."

"It's true, then," Kate answered mournfully. "I have fallen among mountebanks and thieves."

"Not quite true," Grandmother said as she studied her hand carefully. "It's just that not *all* royalty escapes with the country's treasury. My grandfather was too busy with a certain—well, with someone when the crash came, but we managed to escape with a considerable amount of money to... and no, little miss Lenora—it was not the Treasury of Serbia. That had already been spent. So we escaped with money and our wits to support us. And consider, when our earliest ancestor Tsar Boris the First ascended the throne he had really been only a bandit chief. Listen."

"I don't hear anything," Kate replied after a quiet moment.

"Of course you don't," Grandmother said. "That's what I meant. There's no sound. No dogs coughing, no wind blowing—unusual. Nora, you run up to bed now."

"But Grand——"

"Lenora!" The little girl hopped up as if someone had applied a hot iron to her foot. She stood perfectly still until she had mastered all her objections, and then curtsied and ran for the stairs.

"Most old-fashioned," her grandmother mused as she watched the child. "She grows like a weed. The old courtesies help keep her in hand. Now then, child——" Kate hobbled around the table to help the old woman rise. They each took a look at the other, and both giggled. "The blind leading the blind," Grandmother said. "Now then, your instructions. There are only two people who can steal past our dogs, and I am one of them. Ergo, someone is outside who the dogs know very well."

The matriarch chuckled to herself, and took Kate's arm. "I should have brought a cane," she said. "But that's what pride does to one. Now, little one——" Kate, who topped the old lady by a good six inches, stifled another laugh. The old lady tapped her wrist; just a little pat, it looked to be, but the fingers snapped like the end of a bullwhip. "We must remember our manners, child. Er—what was I saying?"

"Now, little one," Kate reminded her as she rubbed her sore wrist.

"Yes. Now, little one, this intruder must be coming to see you. And you will obviously prefer to see him alone. So you may help me up the stairs and see that I get settled, after which you shall come down again and set yourself—ah, on that big stuffed rocking chair—that would be best, and wait for him."

"And wait for him?" Kate was beginning to feel like fresh bait for the lions at the Colosseum. "Wait for him who? What shall I do if——?"

"You'll think of something," Grandmother said gently. "Do what comes naturally. Within reason, of course," she added judiciously.

Kate, feeling as thoroughly over-directed as any movie star might, almost swallowed her tongue. But she finally mastered herself, offered her arm again, and carried out the instructions.

Back downstairs by nine o'clock, she curled herself up in the indicated chair, and tried to settle down, to no avail. Someone who knew all the dogs as well as— Grandmother? It was her first use of the title, and she felt somewhat embarrassed. Someone who would want to see her? Someone whom she would like to see alone? She shook her head. There's no doubt about it, she told herself, ever since I first met this Lee family I've lost at least half my marbles. But if it *is* who I think it is I don't want to meet him dressed in these crummy pants and this apron.

Which is why the loveable Miss Lovewell was just hobbling down the stairs fifteen minutes later, dressed in her one long sheer yellow nightgown with the matching peignoir over it, only to find the intruder had already broken in. And to demonstrate his brass he had put out the living-room lights and was rocking gently back and forth in *her* chair.

"Well," Kate grumbled as she stopped in the doorway. "You've got your nerve!"

"C'mon, Kate," the voice she knew so well said. "I've had a hard day."

"*You've* had a hard day! Say listen, you rotten little— big—Croatian, you don't have any idea of what *hard* really is!"

"Now what?" The words seemed to float on some moving current in the darkness. "You sound as if you might possibly be angry with me."

"You'd better believe it," she said in fury. "You disappear off the face of the earth just as all my enemies seem to be gathering to do me in. And not a word of explanation!''

"It just *seems* that way, Kate. Come over here.''

"Not on your ever-loving life,'' she snapped. "If you want I'll get a kitchen knife and *then* I'll come over there!''

"Now Kate.'' She heard the chair squeak as he stood up. Apprehensively she drew back into the shadowed doorway, her mouth suddenly parched.

"Don't come near me. Not another step nearer!'' She stepped back into the kitchen, and found a convenient broom handle. "I'll brain you if——''

"You couldn't,'' he said. His voice was hypnotic, as dark as the world from which he spoke. "You know you couldn't, Kate Lovewell.''

"Don't kid yourself,'' she snarled, squeezing the broom handle with all her strength.

"*I'm* not the one who's kidding,'' he said. "Love arms, and disarms. You love me, Kathleen, and you know it. Come over here.''

"I don't,'' she sobbed. "I don't, do you hear me? I'm no puppet whose strings you can pull. Go on back to Serbia, why don't you, and haunt a castle?''

"That's Transylvania you're thinking of. And a very distant relative known as Vlad the Impaler.'' A dry chuckle enveloped her. "There's no use fighting it, Kate. Come to me.''

"I will not,'' Kate said fiercely, but even as she said it her feet were moving reluctantly in his direction. "I will not!''

"You will, Kate. Because you want to. Come!''

"You must think me mad or stupid or something,'' she muttered. Her feet were still moving. No matter how often she commanded them to stop, they moved.

"I think you're beautiful," he whispered. Only the whisper was necessary. She was already within touching distance, and his arms closed around her and drew her that last few inches. "You are beautiful," he repeated as he tilted her chin up and sealed her mouth with his lips. "Beautiful, lovely, loveable."

She managed to turn her head away, and raised one hand to cover his mouth. "Don't tell me what you don't mean," she said, sighing. "Maybe I do love you, damn you, but I don't *like* you! Leave me——"

But he was not about to leave her alone. Gently, but as firmly as a closing vice, he trapped both her hands against her body. She made an inarticulate protest. He freed one of his arms; it went around her shoulders with the hand planted squarely in the middle of her back. The fire and temptation of him warmed her through the thin linen of her nightgown, and then suddenly it was not warmth but searing torture as his fingers traced circles in the middle of her back and then walked down to her hips.

"Don't," she muttered. "I don't——"

"Love isn't cold porcelain," he interrupted. "It's fire and emotion and wildness." And as he talked he turned her slightly, and his hand came around to tempt and touch the tip of her breast. "See that?"

She didn't *see*. At the veriest touch she felt the surge of energy flash through her system as her breast grew hard and the bronze nipple stood to attention. Her body shivered uncontrollably, and it was the shaking that *he* felt. He laughed, almost gloated, as his hand brushed aside both peignoir and nightgown and cupped the fullness of her.

"Don't," she protested weakly as her head spun and her reason was shaken by the violence of her own reaction. He laughed again as he swept her up in his arms and fumbled through the darkness in the direction of the couch. As if he were far away she heard him curse as he stumbled over a footstool, and then he dropped her gently on to the massive couch.

For a moment she felt coldness as his body moved away from hers, and then he was back, warmer than before. She knew without touching him that his shirt was gone and her nightgown was being swept aside. His tongue laved her nipple; his teeth nibbled. She moaned again, writhing and squirming as, just for an instant, she felt the sharp prickling of hair as some not-quite-shaven segment of his chin scraped across her breast. Her whole body shook as his lips chased a kiss down over her stomach, past her navel, and then back up to seize her lips again.

She gasped as the muscles of her loins contracted. He stole her tongue and plundered her mouth, and then drew back for a moment and chuckled. It was a tactical mistake. There was just enough of silence and chill and fear to plunge her back into logic. "Don't," she said more firmly.

"You don't mean that," he murmured as he renewed his attack. "I knew you couldn't help yourself."

It was enough, and more. With a burst of her muscular self she broke free from him and pushed his head away. A cool breeze bathed her, adding to her strength. "I said no."

He froze in position in the darkness for just a moment, and then one finger explored her cold face and neck. All her trembling had ceased. Anger had replaced passion. "You really *do* mean it, don't you?" he mused. "I can't believe it!"

"Believe it," she growled at him. "Get off me, you—damn Croatian!"

"A-ha," he grunted. "My grandmother is here."

"And all your rotten ancestors," she snarled. "Get off me!" He moved. Slowly, regrettably, puzzled, but he moved.

Kate swung herself up to her feet, and fumbled with her nightgown. "Love is not enough?" he taunted from a safe distance.

"That isn't love," she snapped. "That's plain, downright lust."

"They're both part of the same thing," he said, sighing. "Love without lust is only an imitation. You don't need another friend, you need a lover."

"As it happens," she said coldly, "I don't need either one. When I do I'll put an advertisement in the local papers. And at its end the ad will say, 'No Croatians need apply.'"

"Wow," he said. "What did I do wrong?"

"It all depends on your definition of wrong," she replied. "Although I admire your grandmother, I think the house of Karageorgeovic must have been a collection of pirates. You knew, of course, that the sheriff plans to auction off my farm tomorrow?"

"Tomorrow? I thought not until the day after."

"A falling out among thieves," she commented acidly. "You probably deserve it."

"What the hell are you talking about now?" he muttered. His big hands closed on her shoulders and gave her a good shake, enough to rattle her brainpan around.

"You know what I'm talking about, Mr. Lee. Just suppose you tell me the truth one time. Are you or are you not Colonel Fessenden's lawyer?"

Deep in darkness, she could see nothing of him except his shadow, but Kate would have sworn that he muttered something along the lines of "Oh, my God!"

"Well? Have you had enough time to think up a good lie?"

"I wouldn't lie to you, Kate."

"Ha! That's all you've ever done since we met. Answer the question; are you Colonel Fessenden's lawyer?"

"Well——" She could feel his hesitation. "No, I'm not. Not exactly," he replied.

"And just what does that mean?"

"That means that the colonel is just what he seems— a noisy busybody without enough sense to organize a scam like this."

"So——" Kate felt the light of inspiration. The colonel was a bumbling busybody? So who else was there to organize any kind of a crooked scheme, and require the best lawyer in the "Newnited States," as Nora told it? The recollection brought a little chuckle, but no relief.

"No, of course not," she said. "You're Mrs. Fessenden's lawyer, aren't you?"

"Yes, so all right," he muttered. "I'm Mrs. Fessenden's lawyer. But it's not what you think, Kate."

"No, I'm sure it isn't," she said. "I'm sure all these little additions are your own idea. Setting yourself up in my house to keep up to all my defenses, trying your best to turn me into your kept woman—your private whore. God, I hate you."

"Kate?"

"Look, by tomorrow night you'll have it all and I'll have nothing. I hope you get someone in here to take care of Nora, so she——" A sudden jolt of comprehension struck Kate at just that moment. And it was just like the damned opinionated man! "Ah," she said.

"That's why your grandmother arrived so suddenly. To take Nora out of this mess! I should have seen it all. It was all there in black and white, written large on the wall, and dumb Katie Lovewell—trusting Katie Lovewell—she couldn't see past the tip of her nose. All right, Mr. Lee, I know the pattern now. It's almost twelve o'clock. Please get yourself off my property. At least I'm entitled to one last night's sleep in the old homestead."

"Kate, I——"

"Just get out," she said wearily. "Get out. Now. And if I don't see you again in this century I'll count myself lucky!" Kate wheeled around, her back to him, to block out the tears. And when she had cleared her eyes enough she turned back slowly. He was gone.

She stumbled on the stairs, not because of the tears, of course, but because of her sore leg. But when she fell into bed the tears really came—in bucketfuls. When she woke up in the morning her sheets were all crumpled and wet, and Nora lay beside her, holding her hand tightly as if the little girl feared she was losing something precious.

Kate managed to drag herself downstairs by about ten o'clock. Grandmother Lee was standing at the foot of the stairs, beaming up at her. As soon as she saw Kate's disgruntled appearance her own smile vanished. "Your leg still hurts, child?"

"Among other things," Kate said glumly. The little grandmother took her arm and escorted her out into the kitchen. Nora was busy at the stove, making a stack of pancakes. She looked up at Kate, and then ducked her head without saying a word.

"Good morning, Nora."

The child brightened visibly. "Oh, we're still speaking?"

"Why, of course we are, love."

"In spite of the dirty tricks my dad has been playing?"

"In spite of," Kate said, and walked over for her daily hug. "See? Children are not responsible for the deficiencies of their parents."

"Well, I'm glad to hear that, whatever that means, 'cause my dad, he struck out completely last night."

"Ah. It sounds as if some little pitchers were sticking noses in," Grandmother commented. "Is this what the volunteering to make breakfast is?"

"No such thing," Nora said suddenly, but she ducked her head again.

"So just where were you when you heard?" Kate said casually.

"Oh, just at the foot of the stairs...darn you, Kate, you're worse than a mother! I wasn't going to tell you that."

"I've been practicing," Kate teased. "I can see that mothering is not all that easy."

"Then you—he——" It was a time for honesty.

"No, sweet. There is no 'you and he' any more. You were right. Your father struck out last night." Kate slumped into her chair at the table, and dabbed at her own eyes. It was going to be hard, learning to live without Jack—and his daughter; but there it was. The three of them started to eat as if their forks were moving to the tempo of the *Funeral March*.

The meal was topped off by a knock at the door. One of the guards, complete with dog, came in. "What is it, Wroclau?" Grandmother asked.

"A deputy from the sheriff's office," Wroclau reported pleasantly. "My dog didn't like him, which seemed to be a nice thing at the time. He made a large number of noises about what he was empowered to do, so I thought you might wish to deal with him."

"Indeed I would," Grandmother Lee said. "Come in, young man. Come in, and tell us your troubles."

"Deputy Sheriff Paine," Kate murmured as Paine came warily to the table. His shiny new uniform was dusty, the corner of his highly polished boots bore the marks of fangs. Altogether Deputy Paine looked as if he would have been happier elsewhere. He edged forward toward a chair. The dog close behind him growled. The deputy jumped up as if he had been bitten, and stood at attention.

"Well?" Grandmother had assumed her regal attitude. Paine edged another inch or two away.

"I have this order," he muttered. "An auction of everything on the farm, land and goods and all."

"I see. Then perhaps you could show me this—order?"

"I don't have to do that!" For a minute the town bully flared up, and went down as quickly as the dog came up to his feet and bared his teeth. "I mean, I'm not supposed to show a court order to every Tom, Dick, and Harry."

"No, of course not, but how about every Kathleen?" Kate interjected. "Since I'm the owner who's being dispossessed, surely I get to see the order?"

"Mr. Bledsoe, he told me I wasn't to show it to anybody," the deputy muttered.

"Ah. Mr. Bledsoe? A lawyer?" Paine nodded his head, and then cringed as the dog sniffed around his heel. "Then perhaps we can expect that you want something else?" The deputy gave an affirmative nod.

"Wroclau," Grandmother Lee ordered, "bring in another one of the dogs, would you please? Mr. Paine seems somewhat uncooperative." The words were enough. Paine, looking as if the words hurt him, hurriedly said, "Mr. Bledsoe wanted me to sort out the best equipment and set it aside for himself when he comes to the auction."

"And when will that be?" The Princess of Serbia had dissolved into somebody's kindly grandmother. The deputy took a deep breath, as if breathing had not been a common thing in his life lately.

"They're coming today, right after one o'clock," he gobbled. "Listen, I'd better go——"

"Perhaps we should hear more about all this," Grandmother said sweetly. "Sheriffs' auctions have to be advertised. There has to be a legal time for inspection before——"

"Please, Grandmother——" Kate put one hand on the old lady's arm. "I know you're doing all this for me, and I appreciate it, but——"

"But you wanna give it up, Kate?" Nora looked over the table grimly. "All your past, and all your future, and you just want to give it up?"

"It doesn't seem to matter," Kate said. Her deep sigh told the entire story. "There's no sense in battling for another day, or hour. I'll miss all my past, little love, but I don't have any future. Let it go."

She slumped back down into her chair, hands in her lap, a look of resignation on her face. Grandmother Lee pursed her lips as she thought. And then a quick gleam of enjoyment sparked from her eyes. Nora, who was about to protest again, received a short snappy sit-down.

"Well, in that case, Deputy Paine," Nora's grandmother said, "I guess we will not try to stand in your way. An auction of all the land and equipment, beginning at one o'clock today?''

"Yes, ma'am," Deputy Paine said. "Can I go now?" They all watched as Mr. Wroclau escorted the still-shaking official over to the door and out on to the steps. For a moment silence reigned. Up until Nora said, "I don't believe it, Kate. I never thought you was a quitter."

"Were a quitter," her grandmother corrected her absentmindedly. "Were a quitter." A pause for further consideration. "Now Nora, you go call in all our young men. Have them leave the dogs on station. And then I'll No, I hate to use that instrument of torture. No, after you call the men in, you make a telephone call to your Uncle Vanya. Here is his address." She handed the girl a crumpled piece of paper.

"What do I tell him?" Nora looked perplexed. "I didn't know he was in Front Royal."

"That's *two* questions, young lady. He's in Front Royal because I told him to go there."

"And what is the message?"

"Why, tell him to come here." And then, anticipating another question, "Because I want him here."

"Yes, ma'am." The little girl left the table and rushed for the door, stopping only when her grandmother cleared her throat loudly. At which noise Nora skidded to a stop, turned, and offered the briefest curtsy the world had ever seen.

"She'll do." Grandmother Lee smiled with some satisfaction. "And so will you, loveable Kate Lovewell. Now——"

"Me?" Kate's spirit was so low she would have had to look up to see a snake's belly pass by.

"You," Grandmother Lee said. "You have size and shape and beauty, but you need a little more instruction in chicanery. And that we will begin immediately. I'd like to kill that grandson of mine. Where was I?''

"You'd like to kill that—you can't do that!''

"Of course I can't,'' the regal charmer said. "I'm saving that for you, no? Now, here's what we shall do.'' And she explained it all slowly and carefully, until even Kate started to chuckle.

CHAPTER NINE

THE auctioneer arrived just after lunch. He was a professional from outside Luray. "Jake Weathers," he introduced himself. "Friend of your father's I was, little lady. Your dad and me was at school together. Best of friends, as I remember. Up till the time he married *my* girlfriend. Lovely lady, your ma. And now you have to sell out?"

"I'm afraid so," Kate said. Little lady? His must be a memory that stretches way back! "I—don't understand any of this, but my lawyer said that it's——"

"Bledsoe? A snake in the grass," Weathers interrupted emphatically. "And this be your...grandmother?"

"Absolutely right." Not the matriarch this time, but somebody's hill-country granny. She came out and stood beside Kate, putting an arm around the girl's slender waist. "This is a public auction? You wouldn't mind if a few of us bid—on the smaller things, of course?"

"Don't mind a'tall," he said. "As you say, a public auction. But, let me tell you, the craziest auction I've ever seen. Only gave me twenty-four hours' advance notice, they did. If it wasn't for the fact the place is run down, I'd think..." He paused in midsentence, and chewed on the wooden toothpick that seemed to be perpetually in his mouth.

"You'd think?" Grandmother Lee prodded.

"I'd think this was as phony as a three-dollar bill," he opined. "Got to have a crowd to make a successful

159

auction. Ain't seen nothin' but the little newspaper ad from up Front Royal away. That's a long way from here. Folks like to be able to drive around, look things over before they bid. And you know sumpin' strange? According to this equipment list they give me, you ain't got enough stuff around to farm one acre."

"That's the way of it when somebody has to hurry," Grandmother said. "Perhaps we could help? We still have three or four hands available. They might check your list against what's in the barns? Or maybe the rest of the equipment is—how do you say——? Ah, Vanya! May I present my oldest son, Vanya, Mr. Weathers?"

Uncle Vanya was playing some part—Kate was not quite sure which one. The old plantation owner? He was dressed in a three-piece white suit, with a flower in his lapel. A wide-brimmed black hat covered his bald spot.

"Folks call me Jake, ma'am. Vanya?" Two hands, almost as big and tough as each other, met in a shake. "Vanya? Ain't heard that kind of name before in these parts. You a foreigner?"

"I guess you might say that," Uncle Vanya said. "What made you suspect?"

"Easy. In Virginia people talk *real* English."

"Of course," Grandmother chuckled. "Everything outside Virginia is foreign."

"You jus' bet," Jake laughed. "You been to one of them la-de-dah schools, I suspect."

"Hit it right on the head," Uncle Vanya admitted. "Graduated from one of those back-country schools called Balliol. Heard of it, have you?"

"Might have," Jake said. "Somewheres up north?"

"Can't fool you," Vanya said, chuckling. "Say, look, instead of all this searching around, why don't you give me the list, and I'll have the equipment brought out in the sunshine? Be easier to handle that way."

"That's my son," Grandmother Lee interjected proudly. "Always was brighter than the average Karageorgeovic."

"Well, look here," Jake commented. "Here comes the crowd."

As crowds went, this one wasn't much. Two patrol cars from the sheriff's department. One limousine containing Mrs. Fessenden and a man sitting back in the corner, almost invisible. One car each for Bledsoe and for Gerney, the legal team, and a car for the bank representative. "Although I don't know why he would come," Kate whispered. "Our house mortgage was paid off in 1884. I've got the framed receipt hanging on the wall in the living room."

"Shush. I think we're about to begin."

Jake's name was accurate. He was a weather-beaten and somewhat bent mountain man. In normal conversation his voice was a raspy whisper that seemed almost ready to give out. But when he climbed up on the seat of the buggy that Grandmother's guards had just wheeled out, and started his chant, he could be heard for half a mile around.

Mrs. Fessenden came around the front of the limousine, heading for a position at the front. Kate barely caught the disgusted look on the woman's face, and then shrank back to the side of the buggy. The man behind Mrs. Fessenden was Jack Lee. Bile rose in Katie's throat, bile and anger and fear and—good heavens, could it still be love? She followed his every move as he came up behind his client, and began to whisper in her ear. Somehow all the sounds around her faded. Everything had turned into a silent movie, but only for a moment.

"No, I don't think I can do that," Jake was saying. "Got everything orderly on my list, and that's the way I mean to sell it."

"I don't want to stand around while you sell off this junk," Mrs. Fessenden wailed.

"Junk?" Jake looked back at his list. "Says here this junk is worth nigh on to seventy thousand dollars. Got a reserve figure, at that. Prices can't go below the reserve, and there ain't nobody but the present owner can waive the reserve price. And that is Ms. Lovewell."

Somebody was breathing excitedly in Kate's ear. "Waive it," Vanya said. "Waive everything."

"I waive the reserve figures on everything," Kate yelled, and then wondered why she had done so. It pleased Grandmother. It pleased Uncle Vanya. It almost seemed, from this distance, that even Jack Lee was smiling, pleased. What have I done wrong now? Kate asked herself. Something stupid, no doubt about that!

Jake went back to his high-speed chant, asking for the first bid on the buggy. "Twenty-five," Uncle Vanya called.

"That's the way," Jake encouraged him. "Twenty-five hundred dollars." His little hammer slammed on the back of the seat. "Who'll give me twenty-six?"

"You've got that wrong," Vanya yelled. "That's twenty-five cents."

It looked for a minute as if Jake had swallowed his toothpick. "Twenty-five cents for this fine antique buggy? It's worth fifty dollars as a museum piece. Who'll give me twenty-six?"

Kate peered around the side of the buggy. All the participants had gathered in a tiny crowd. All four of Grandmother's guards were stationed at strategic points surrounding them. Each guard had brought his Doberman from wherever they had been hidden.

The dogs were impatient, and had to be restrained. Despite the leashes the animals were sniffing at shoes, giving warning growls.

"That'll do it," Kate whispered to Grandmother Lee. "Mr. Bledsoe is chairman of the museum. He's bound to——"

"Twenty-five dollars," Bledsoe yelled.

"Ah, that's better," Jake crowed. "Now we're going. Mr.—Bledsoe, you bid twenty-five dollars?" There was a loud silence from the center of the crowd. Kate had to stretch up on tiptoes to see what was going on. Grandmother Lee was too short to see at all, and it aggravated her. Lawyer Bledsoe was having trouble, too. The moment he announced his bid one of the Dobermans raced toward him, stood at practically no distance away, and growled. A moment later a second dog came racing through the crowd, his own handler barely able to keep up on the leash. The guards said something under their breath to Bledsoe; the dogs said something under their breath to the lawyer. Something on the order of "Make another bid and I'll tear your throat out." Or so Bledsoe seemed to interpret it.

"Not me," he bleated. "Not me. I'm not bidding, just clearing my throat."

"Well, in that case," Jake Weathers concluded mournfully, "I got one bid on this fine buggy, twenty-five cents. Who'll make it thirty? Twenty-five, going once, going twice...sold to the gentleman with the moustache." His little hammer bounded off the buggy seat, and it seemed that everyone sighed. Uncle Vanya brushed at his tiny moustache, and grinned at his mother. Who promptly grinned back.

The afternoon moved slowly forward. Jake Weathers worked his way up through the longest pile of junk anyone could wish for. Several times Vanya and his mother would bid against each other, driving the price up a penny or two at each call. Mrs. Fessenden stirred her anger, and made long complaint, after which one of the guards was sent off for a chair. The auction dragged on.

But Jack Lee never said a word. Kate kept herself behind the buggy, glancing from Grandmother to Jack, working herself up into a frenzy. There was only one interruption. At about three o'clock in the afternoon Nora came out on to the porch. The little girl watched for perhaps ten minutes, then stomped across the grass to stand in front of her father, both hands on her hips, a mutinous scowl on her face. She said something to him, something very short. He gave a one-word reply. Nora shrugged her shoulders, then kicked her father in the shin with one of her sharp-pointed shoes. He shifted his weight to the other foot, and made some indistinguishable retort, but Nora had already left.

Jack Weathers halted the auction. All the audience was watching the girl, anyway. She walked straight across to Kate, gave her an affectionate hug, and turned to her uncle. Her voice was loud enough to be heard throughout the crowd. "Uncle Vanya, I wanna get a divorce from my father. Can you help me?"

A buzz of conversation rustled through the crowd. Her uncle bent down on one knee and conducted a quiet conference with his niece. Kate exhaled. She had been holding her breath for what seemed like hours. But Uncle Vanya, she knew, would be both direct and patient with the girl. Can you divorce your parents? Kate asked herself. And select someone else? What a great idea!

"Well, now, that's all the odds and ends of things," Jake said. "Why don't we get this auction on the road? The next item on the list is one house, and two barns. We'll sell them off as a unit. Who'll bid—ten thousand dollars?"

"Ten thousand dollars," Mrs. Fessenden shouted.

"Ten thousand dollars. I have ten thousand. Eleven thousand?"

Mrs. Fessenden stood up and glared around her. The guards and the dogs made no attempt to interfere. Grandmother Lee, who had been sitting on the buggy seat, took Vanya's arm and stood up. All eyes turned in her direction. She coughed, looked around with the most gentle of expressions on her face, and said, "Five hundred thousand dollars." And quietly sat down again.

The silence was so loud and long that it must have been heard as far away as Richmond. Deep, deadly silence! Mrs. Fessenden seemed to waver, and grabbed at the nearest arm to keep herself upright. Jack Lee's arm, Kate noted. *I hope he gets leprosy from it. Or worse, shingles! I wish it was me, holding on there like a mustard plaster!*

"I don't think she's got twenty cents," Mrs. Fessenden yelled. A car drove up behind her, a middle-aged Buick, with the colonel at the wheel. The dapper colonel crawled out, looking neither dapper nor young. He hurried over to his wife. "I demand she show she's got the money," his wife was yelling. Jack Weathers pounded his gavel for silence. Colonel Fessenden whispered something in his wife's ear. She seemed staggered by whatever it was she had been told. The dominating scowl on her face fled before an attack of fright. She turned pale, and collapsed in her chair again. Another car drove up.

"Well, ma'am," Jake said. "You got that kinda money?"

"I have a few pennies," Grandmother Lee said. "Four or five bank drafts, each for fifty thousand dollars." She fumbled around in her massive leather pocketbook, and came out with a handful of papers. "I always like to carry a little pin money with me. Would that be enough?"

"Lady, was you wantin' to bid on the State House that would be enough." Jake's interest in his toothpick suddenly seemed to desert him. He struggled for a minute. "I got five hundred thousand," he chanted, slamming down on his little hammer. "Do I hear six?"

A third car drove up. Altogether now, Kate thought, we've attracted six state troopers, the county sheriff himself, and two or three miscellaneous dark-suited men whom she could not identify. And, while Colonel Fessenden did his best to comfort his weeping wife, Jack Lee walked over to the sheriff, standing by the auctioneer, and they conferred. It seemed that Jack was doing the speaking, the sheriff was doing the nodding, and Jake Weathers, once every thirty seconds was saying either "You don't say?" or "Well, I'll be dinged!"

The two lawyers, Bledsoe and Gerney, trying to appear like casual passersby, began to slide out of the middle of the crowd, only to find themselves confronted by two very large policemen. "Don't be in a hurry," the legal beagles were told. "There's plenty of entertainment to come."

Sheriff Baker climbed up on the buggy, and called for attention. "For those who don't know," he announced, "I am the county sheriff. It is my special pleasure to announce to you that this auction is illegal, and is hereby canceled." The several spectators began to fade away. "No, don't rush off," the sheriff said.

"I have here in my pocket some bench warrants. If you young men over there would arrest Mrs. Fessenden—that lady behind all the tears in that chair. Ma'am, you are under arrest, charged with conspiracy to defraud. Along with these two lawyers over here. Got them? That's nice, what you young people can do. Take them in to Stanfield, and lock them up until Judge Pettibone can get around to them." The sheriff stopped to check off a couple more names on his list of wants and warrants.

"And now you there—with the dog—yes, you. You're standing right next to Deputy Sheriff Paine, for whom I have a warrant charging malfeasance in office, possession of a controlled substance, and possession with intent to sell a controlled substance. I have some more warrants for him, but that ought to do. Yes, sir—you might use his own handcuffs on him. That seems right and proper. And if you will put him in my car over there I'll take him along after a time."

"And what about Colonel Fessenden?" Uncle Vanya asked. "I have a terrible suspicion about men who become colonels without ever being in the military service."

"Well, as best me and the FBI are concerned," the sheriff mused, "there's only two charges against the colonel. One is for keeping dogs without a license——"

"And the other?" Grandmother Lee queried.

"Well, ma'am. The other ain't really a charge. He's been consorting with a known criminal—to wit, Mrs. Fessenden, but the Commonwealth of Virginia cannot legally prosecute him for stupidity. You can leave now,

Colonel." The sheriff carefully climbed down from the buggy. "Arthritis," he commented as he reached out for a helping hand.

"Hey, just wait a minute," Katie yelled. Everyone stopped in place. "You're letting the worst one of them get away. Him." She pointed her finger dead at Jack Lee. "The mastermind of the bunch!"

All those separate people, going in their several directions, stopped for a moment to take in her accusation, and they all began to laugh. The sheriff roared so much that he had to fumble for the chair that Mrs. Fessenden had been using, into which he collapsed. Everybody was laughing, except for Jack Lee and Kate Lovewell; Jack, looking as if he was about to commit murder, was walking angrily in her direction.

Kate, having been born of no stupid parents, hesitated for a second or two, and then took off for the hills behind the barn! In a matter of seconds her mind triumphed over her damaged leg. From a fitful hobble she worked her way up to gazelle speed. And besides, she told herself, in desperation, I know the land, and he's a damn foreigner!

"So, I've finally caught you!" Tackled her, for a fact. Tackled her as she broke out of the trees and tried to make it across the hayloft north of the house.

"You'd better look out," Kate yelled at him as she rolled over, sat up, and started to brush debris from her hair. "The sheriff isn't too far away. I can scream like you've never heard before. They'd lock you up for a hundred years, here in Virginia. Folks around here don't put up with——"

"With what?" he interrupted, his face as grim as the executioner's.

"Attempted rape," she muttered, her mind too far gone for sensible thinking. But then, having caught her breath, she put her intelligence to work. "Assault and battery," she added to the list. "Look, my elbow's bleeding!"

"Damned if that's true," he said. "That's my nose and my blood. What do you have to say to that?"

"Fraud," she said belligerently.

"Fraud? How do you figure fraud?"

"Kissing with intent to deceive," she muttered. "Turn me loose, you damn Croatian bas——"

"No. That's not true." He sat up beside her and shook her, not too gently. "My mother and father were married for two years before I was born. Want to try again?"

"Consorting with the enemy," she blustered. "Conspiracy to defraud." She used both sets of knuckles to clear the tears from her eyes. "Don't you think I saw what you were up to? Don't you think I believe what the colonel told me? I wasn't born yesterday, Mr. Lee. You were Mrs. Fessenden's lawyer long before you became mine." She stopped for another deep breath. Accusing and loving, all at the same time, required a great deal more energy than she was prepared for. "And that, I'm sure, is malpractice, Mr. Lee. Wait'll I call up the county bar association. I'll bet you could be debarred——"

"It's not like de-horning cattle," he interrupted. "You mean I could be disbarred!"

"Just another one of your legal technicalities," she muttered, and the thought turned on her tears almost automatically.

"Don't cry, for God's sake. That's not fair. Enough is enough. I'd think you'd be happy as a clam to see me disbarred. Thrown out of work. Putting my daughter on welfare. Shaming my grandmother's fair name?''

"Oh, God," she wailed, and the drip of tears turned into a waterfall.

"Oh, God? You wouldn't want to see me ruined?"

"About *you* I don't care a darn," she managed. "But Grandmother and Nora, that's a different story! *You* they could put away for years and years, and it would never stir a tear. What are you doing?"

"I'm addressing the first charge," he murmured. Suddenly they were both sitting up, facing in opposite directions, and his arms were around her, pulling her over to lean against him.

It was close to six o'clock, and a cool wind was starting to blow up the valley. But his touch, his envelopment cut off the chill. She relaxed against his warm chest, relaxed her muscles, let her whole weight fall on his arms and against his shoulder. One of his hands came up and brushed her hair out of her eyes. She stared at him, a rabbit hypnotized by a hawk. "What——?" she managed to whisper.

"Kissing with intent to defraud," he said softly. Her mouth half opened to protest, and he sealed her up with his lips. Warmth and moisture, an insistent pressure as his tongue penetrated her mouth and set his mark on her. Kate struggled for a microsecond, and then collapsed into the enjoyment of it. His one hand stroked her hair gently; the other held her in his kissing trap. He could have done *that* with two fingers, she told herself wildly as she came to life.

There was a need running wild in her mind. A need to be closer, to explore, but her position, sitting beside him on the grass, was not helpful. She managed to wiggle her way up and into his lap. "Oh, Jack," she murmured during that second or two while her mouth was clear of him.

And now he was not holding *her* at all. Her own hands had come up around his neck, her body turned slightly so that she pressed against the steel of his chest, her tongue seeking, finding.

"Oh, Jack," somebody sighed. His free hand was at her waist, exploring the hem of her blouse. Slipping under it to rest for a moment on the soft bulge of her hip, and then wandering up, tantalizing, toward the swell of her unfettered breast. And then everything came to a halt.

She cried out for a moment against the loss of warmth, the cessation of wild sensations. He was pushing her slightly away from him. "Oh, no," she pleaded.

"Oh, yes," he corrected. "Kissing with intent to defraud?"

"No." A tremendous sigh shook her body. He felt it more than she did. "No," she said. "Not guilty." And then a pause as she struggled for control. "Why did this happen to me? I've been a nice girl for years and years, and now look at me! I love you, Jack Lee, even if you're the most dangerous uncaught bandit east of the Mississippi. Why me, God?"

"That's a good start," he commented as he helped her up to her feet. "Now, if I can get you back to the house we'll see if we can sort this whole thing out."

Kate looked down at the crushed grass, the soft and perfect nest they had shared for too short a time. "Maybe we'd better wait until the sheriff leaves the house," she suggested. "I wouldn't want you arrested before you do this major miracle—explaining all this away, I mean!" Maybe we could wait out here as long as tomorrow, hoping it won't rain? Hayfields are famous in history for use in this sort of . . . I wish I knew what you really call it. Queen Victoria certainly ruined a large and interesting part of the language!

"No stalling," he said, interrupting her wonderful little daydream. "Back to the house. My grandmother doesn't approve of an unmarried couple doing things in a hayfield."

"What things?" she challenged.

"Those things that both you and I are thinking about doing if we don't get up and out of here," he told her as he snatched up her hand and started off in the general direction of the house. Kate Lovewell dreamed all the way home.

"You're supposed to carry her, Daddy." Nora stamped her foot in disgust. They were all gathered around the dining-room table—Grandmother Lee, Uncle Vanya, and Nora. But when Kate tried to move away from the feast which Nora had prepared her leg was so stiff that she could not move it.

"You can see she's hurt," Nora insisted. "She wasn't that bad off when you chased her into the trees."

"How lucky I am to have such an observant child," Jack said sarcastically. "And if I pick her up I'll have a strained back. You don't seem to have any idea how much the lady weighs!"

"Don't bother," Kate growled. "I'd crawl before I'd let that man lay a hand on me. On my hands and knees I'd crawl!"

"Everybody clear out of the way," Jack announced. "We're about to——"

At the head of the table the little old lady, dressed in starchy black with white Belgian lace running from here to forever, tapped twice with her spoon against her glass.

The little tinkle brought the entire discussion to a close. With a dozen well-chosen Serbo-Croatian words one could almost see the diadem resting within the crown of her white hair. Her son Vanya gasped. "Mama!" he cautioned. Her grandson John shut his mouth carefully, as if afraid he might break the hinge of his jaw. Her great-granddaughter Nora covered her mouth with both her hands to keep the giggles from leaking through. And without any further debate Jack came over to the table, carefully turned Kate's chair, lifted her out of it, and carried her through to the living room, where he deposited her oh, so gently on the sofa. He took a step backward to admire his work, grinning, but another spurt of Croatian wiped the grin away.

"Now?" he asked. "She's been insulting me all day."

"So would I," his grandmother said. "Now!"

The last gentle word cracked like the tip of a bull-whip. As big a man as he was, Kate could see him flinch. He came back to the couch, reached down for her hand, and treasured it. "My grandmother," he said, "instructs me to tell you how sorry I am to have been such a stupid——" He stopped, and glanced across at the matriarch. She nodded her head in a commanding gesture. He turned back to Kate again. She shifted uneasily, trying to move an additional inch away from him. But he looked so—loveable that she lost her sense of fear. "Where was I?" he asked.

"Sorry that you were such a stupid," Kate suggested very meekly.

"Yes. That I have been such a stupid jackass." And then he treasured her hand in his once more, and bent over and kissed its palm. There was silence from the group, and then a round of applause. Under cover of the noise he leaned closer and whispered, "Actually, she didn't say jackass, but the word she *did* use was... untranslatable."

"Eating humble pie?" She was whispering, as he had been on that last exchange. "Now you're going to tell me that your grandmother is queen of the roost, and you're a downtrodden beat-upon male!"

"I couldn't have said it better myself," he said, with all his usual cockiness. "Now, Uncle Vanya, why don't you tell the young lady about my exploits?"

"It wouldn't do to be caught blowing your own horn? Well, all right. Actually, Miss Lovewell—er—are you actually going to marry this big oaf?"

"I ... haven't been asked," Kate retorted.

"Well then, Katie," he said, chuckling. "We operate a corporate business. My mother is the financial whizz, I do all the detecting, and my nephew here does all the thinking. So it didn't take us long to see what the focal point of the problem was—is? Sometimes I have trouble with the little English words still. So; the new development in this area will undoubtedly start right where your farm is. And the person who knew this, besides the developer, was Mrs. Fessenden. Who, by the way, is the brains in her family. The two lawyers were working at the legal aspects, the deputy sheriff responded more simply to money."

"But why couldn't the information have leaked out from the developer?" Kate asked.

"Later," Vanya replied. "Later." He scratched the tip of his nose, replaced his glasses, and continued. "So the first step was to get your father into a mess about money. The answer again was money. A gambling operation was set up, in which your father was the only—er—"

"Pigeon," Jack furnished.

"Yes, pigeon," Vanya said. "Now your father was very distracted at the time. The death of your mother, I presume. In any event they took him for a great deal of money. Peter Lester was the kingpin of this affair. And he has agreed to testify to that concern."

"Peter?" Out of the corner of her eye Kate could see the quick frown that flashed across Jack's face at the happy sound. Kate used both her hands to trap Jack's. "I only thought it was—you know—righting a wrong he had done us, confessing and all that. I'm sure God would erase a few of the black spots on his character."

"Yes, I'm sure He will," Vanya agreed. "Just as soon as poor Peter's broken jaw heals."

"Oh, my," Kate offered. Out of the corner of her eyes he could see Jack turning his hand over so that she couldn't see the back of it, and his bruised knuckles.

"Well, anyway," Vanya continued, "the major problem was getting the evidence, the warrants—all that paperwork that the law requires. So when we discovered that the foreclosure had been declared, and the auction scheduled, why, my nephew John volunteered to act as the decoy to delay them. He went over and volunteered to be Mrs. Fessenden's adviser."

"Only Grandma had already figured out how to slow things down," Nora said gleefully. "If you really wanna know where all the scheming comes from, there it is." She pointed dramatically across the room at the matriarch.

"Damn it," Jack said mournfully, "*I* was supposed to be the hero of this, and you've blown the works, Miss Nora Lee."

"So then you were busy behind the scenes gathering all this evidence, and stuff like that," Kate mused. He was wearing a terribly shifty look, so she took a wild guess. "That didn't include wining and dining the lady?"

"Of course it did," Jack responded. "Don't you ever read any spy and detective stories?"

"Yes, I read a number of them," Kate said as she shifted her gaze to the blanket he had thrown over her, and began picking at one of the loose threads. "And the thing that bothers me is that the macho hero spends a great deal of his time with the villainess in a horizontal position!"

"Luckily no member of the House of Karageorgeovic would ever consider doing things like that," Grandmother interrupted. "And another thing that will make you happy, Katie. In Virginia gambling is illegal, except when conducted in a state-licensed place of business. And since your father's gambling was conducted in Mrs. Fessenden's house no debts accrued from such action may be collected. With a smart lawyer I think you could recover, oh—Jack?"

"Anything's possible," Jack Lee told her. "Anything from twenty-five dollars to two hundred and fifty thousand. How's that grab you?"

"Oh, Lord, that sounds fine," Kate said, excited. "I can have the rest of the house fixed up and painted, and put the land to some use, to keep those pirates from Washington from turning the valley into a…" Her voice trailed off as she noticed that nobody in the room except herself was smiling.

Uncle Vanya put his hands in his pockets and began to whistle dolefully. Nora backed up until she bumped into her father, and then looked up at him with a worried look on her face. "Papa, is that going to spoil everything?"

"I think, at this point," the matriarch said, "we had best leave everything in my son's hands. Vanya?"

"I have the car. I think I'll start back to Washington now," he said. "I could send the helicopter down for you in the morning?"

"A very excellent idea," Grandmother agreed. "And for now, considering how late it is and how much we've done, I would suggest that you and I, Lenora, go to bed."

"I don't wanna," the little girl snapped. "Everybody's had all their questions asked, and there wasn't none of them as important——"

"Weren't," her father interrupted.

"Weren't none of them important as mine, and why should I have to go off to bed before I find out if——?"

"Go to bed, child," her father commanded. "You're not the only one who wants that answer. Git!"

And so goodbyes were said, cheeks were kissed, Vanya disappeared, and in a moment the smooth sound of his limousine motor could be heard. Nora stood for a moment at the foot of the stairs, and then, with her great grandmother's hand on her shoulder for support, labored up the stairs, chattering away like a finch in the nest at daybreak.

"And that," Jack Lee said, "leaves only one question to be answered."

"No, that's not true," Kate said. "I have a question." She moved over to make room for him to sit on the porch.

"In all this weaving and boxing, Mr. Lee, we kept bouncing around the question about how did Mrs. Fessenden find out about the land business?"

"I don't know," he lied. She pressed him. "Well," he finally admitted, "we employ only Serbs and Croatians in our office. One of them sold us out. His name? Karageorgeovic, of course."

"Reverting to type, was he?" she said, chortling. The corner of his mouth kept twitching. She didn't pursue *that* problem, because she wanted to have some small advantage over him in the years to come. Fifty years or more. The Karageorgeovic family seems to be long lived, doesn't it? It was a good question, so she asked.

"Lord, no!" he exclaimed, startled by the change of subject. "The Karageorgeovic family was a race of scallywags who fast-talked their way on to the throne of Serbia, and then married into the rest of the Slavic kingdoms. They seldom lived long. Assassination was a great form of entertainment back in the good old days. No, the only members of the family that turned out to be long lived were those who took refuge in America."

Kate looked up at him, pursing her lips. So we'll live together for fifty years if I don't assassinate him sooner, she thought. What a lovely idea.

He was staring at her, wondering what was to come next. So she went on. "Back to this development, and all those people you trust implicitly. Who is it that *owns* all this development, in whom you have such absolute trust?"

Jack Lee got up from the couch, and moved away to the open front door. "There'll be a beautiful moon tonight," he said. "Now that I think of it, this would be a wonderful place to raise a family."

"No doubt. The name, please. Who owns this development company?"

"Me," he said glumly. "Just me."

CHAPTER TEN

THE helicopter roared in low over the mountain at ten o'clock. Grandmother Lee was already impatiently waiting on the porch, her bag packed, her rebellious granddaughter not quite in hand.

"But we only got to the int'restin' part," Nora objected. "I wanna stay around and see the ending."

"Your papa will take care of the ending," her grandmother insisted.

"He'll make an awful mess," Nora said stubbornly. "You got any idea how many floozies he brought home and almost got married to, only I wouldn't let him?"

"Floozies?" Grandmother frowned her most regal frown, and then a tiny smile formed. "Some of them were very far-out, were they not, child?"

"He's probably the smartest lawyer in the world," Nora continued, "but he don't know from nothin' about women. He needs a—a keeper."

"There may be something in what you say," Grandmother mused.

"And I like this one," Nora insisted.

"To tell the truth, so do I." The gray eyes blinked at the blue ones, and two smiles appeared. "You have just got a terrible headache," the matriarch said. "The helicopter noises will make it worse. You will probably be sick."

"I do? It will? I would?"

"Yes," her grandmother said. The machine made one more pass over the front yard. Bits of stick and grass and debris were vacuumed up and spread over the adjacent quarter acre. Grandmother Lee stood up, with one hand on Nora's shoulder to provide balance. And at that moment, hurrying from opposite ends of the house, Kate and Jack put in an appearance. The jet engine was throttled back, and the rotor sounds dropped to conversational level. "There is nothing better," the matriarch said, "than having a child who understands without a great deal of explanation."

"I thought I'd be too late to say goodbye," Kate said. "I was upstairs—cleaning the bathroom——" Oh, what a lie, she told herself. I was upstairs crying, that's what. What am I going to do about the Lee family? If the Washington football team had a runner as shifty as Jack Lee they'd be national champions every year. If I give this pirate an inch he'll take a mile. And if I *don't* give him an inch he might just walk off and find someone else! Kate was startled when Grandmother Lee rambled on.

"Lenora has a headache," the matriarch announced. "A very bad headache." Her granddaughter dropped her chin and tried to look miserable. "All of which can only be made worse by a trip in a noisy helicopter." Nora, a consummate actress, like most little girls, managed to winkle out a tear and cover her ears with both hands. "Therefore it will be better for her to remain here. When a girl is feeling sickly there is nothing better for her than the attention of a loving father." Nora, overplaying her part, gagged very realistically, and only stopped when the hand on her shoulder squeezed a little too hard. "Kiss me, child."

Nora stretched, Grandmother Lee bent over slightly, and the deed was done. But it was the regal grandmother who turned to Kate and said, "You too, child. You may kiss me." The conversion from Grandmother to royalty was a little too much for common Kate, but she rubbed her lips with her wisp of a handkerchief, bent over the tiny woman, and complied.

And while her ear was still close to the royal cheek she heard a whisper. "Go get 'im," royalty said in a very plebeian aside.

Jack Lee was a very subdued man as he came back from escorting his grandmother to the chopper. Nora stood on the porch beside Kate, holding her hand and brushing as close as possible to her side.

During the course of the elderly lady's trip to the helicopter, her arm solidly entwined in her grandson's arm, the pair on the porch could see much emphasis with the fingers, the hand, the arm—all from the matriarch. From time to time Jack would nod, but it was obvious that he was not being given time to respond.

"Getting his marching orders," Nora giggled. "There are times my dad thinks he's in charge of the family."

"And he's not?"

"Depends on who he's talkin' to," the girl answered. "But when Grandmother cracks the whip—well!"

"How interesting," Kate reflected as she stowed that tidbit away in the corner of her mind marked "Him." Maybe that's the way to handle him—the imperial way that his grandmother uses!

And then a little touch of ceremony over at the helicopter stairs brought a trace of a tear to Kate's eye. The matriarch extended her hand, her grandson took it, bowed to kiss it, and then stepped back, backbone straight as steel, watching as the crew helped the old lady into the machine. At which he proffered a stiff quarter bow, and stepped away. "And that," Kate said, dabbing at her eye, "is one of the fine little ceremonies we've lost in passing through the years. It might be nice being a princess, pet.''

"Don't you believe it," Nora replied. "For a minute, maybe, but not for life. Grandma had many a scare, many a threat during her life. Revolutions aren't just ice cream and cake. Once I heard her tell my dad about the time in 1916 when the rebels had her and her mother lined up against a wall. Uncle Vanya saved her. No, Europe is still cluttered with ex-royalty, scraping to keep body and soul alive. And you have no idea how many poor noblemen still turn to Grandma for help! Nope. They don't have no pension plan for royalty after the revolution. I'm gladder to be Nora than Lenora.''

"I hadn't thought of it that way," Kate said, brought down from her dream trip in a hurry. "Glad, not gladder,'' she corrected.

"Whatever you say," Nora agreed, and squeezed the hand she was holding. Across the field the helicopter coughed, worked up some enthusiasm, and went roaring away into the brilliant morning sun.

"Thank the Lord," Jack said as he came up the porch steps, wiping perspiration off his brow. "My grand-mother is——"

"Your oldest relative," his daughter interrupted, with a scathing look. He glanced down at her, surprised, and mulled over the comment for a moment.

"Yes," he said solemnly. "My oldest relative. Now then, ladies, except for a few court cases—and that damn clock—I suppose we can get down to routine living.''

"Don't you lay a finger on my clock," Kate threatened.

"Oh, Papa," Nora said, dismayed. "My headache's getting worser." Neither one of the adults, looking at her disgruntled face, dared to offer a correction.

Not until the child had gone upstairs did he dare to say a word. "A fine little lady," he commented. "Just a few more lessons and she'll turn out to be one of the cheekiest ladies on the east coast."

It was just enough to set off Kate's temper. "And who," she declaimed pompously, "do you know who's smart enough to teach her?"

He recognized the danger line and stepped over it jauntily. "My grandmother, for one. And my wife for another."

"Ha! A likely story that is. Who do you know that's fool enough to marry a Croatian bandit?"

He held up his left hand, as if exclaiming his fingernails. "Besides you, you mean?"

"Don't give me that guff," she roared at him. But it was only a halfhearted roar. Behind her beautiful high forehead gears were running at full speed. Besides you?

"Now that *is* a laugh," she retorted weakly, but even *she* could hear the quaver in her voice. He was wearing a lazy sort of smile as he moved closer to her, and dropped a heavy hand on each of her shoulders. One gentle little shake followed.

"Now listen up," he said. "My grandmother gets away with that stuff because I admire and respect her. She's had seventy-five years of——"

"Eighty-five," Kate corrected. Which earned herself another little shake.

"And that's another thing," he muttered. "All that 'I know everything' stuff is just right for my daughter, but from my wife—that is something, lady, up with which I will not put!"

"Winston Churchill said it first," she interjected, and earned herself two more little shakes. Well, perhaps they weren't all that little. He *was* a very big man.

"I can see I have to take you firmly in hand, Kate Lovewell. They were almost nose to nose, but Kate found herself unable to leave it alone. "You and how many brothers will that take?" she demanded.

"Oh, I think I can manage to work my way through the thickets, as we say in Virginia."

"As *we* say in Virginia? Why, you darn carpet-bagger!" She had meant to say something nasty about his parentage, but by the time she had chosen the right words his lips were on hers, the seal was complete, and although she struggled for a second or two they both knew the battle was lost.

Kate closed her eyes, and relaxed within the circle of his arms as his tongue pursued her back into the cave of her mind. He relented long enough to say, "Repeat after me. I love you." And a single little shake.

"Repeat after me. I love you," she murmured, and the warm moist pressure of his lips were back on hers again. It lasted until she had run out of air, until her feet were tingling, until her breasts had snapped to attention and her mind was playing tag on some far pink cloud. And then he stopped again.

"Always a smart aleck," he said softly. "Fight until the last drop of blood. Right?"

"Right. We Lovewells fight on, even after the Confederacy surrendered! It's a wonder there are any of us left."

"I wish I could have known your father." He cuddled her up against his shoulder, using one hand to lock her in place, and the other to course up and down from her hip to her breast. She shuddered in anticipation. "I'm sure there was a lot I could have learned from him." Another kiss, that sent her mind reeling. When he released her her knees could not hold her up. She dropped on to the nearby rocking chair. It took a moment or two for her to work up a facsimile of a frown.

"If you think all this sweet-talking is going to get you all my land to building a gas station on you've got another thought coming, John Lee."

"A-ha! That's the mouse nibbling at the cheese, huh?" He leaned down and picked her up, hugging her closely. "You are indeed a hostile witness," he said, sighing. "Answer yes or no. No buts. No equivocation. Got that?"

"I'll——"

He lifted her a little higher, and gently bit the lobe of her ear. "Yes or no," he repeated as he tossed her up in the air.

"I get seasick easy..."

"Yes or no. Got it." He faked another toss up into the air. She gasped and clung more closely to him.

"Yes," she whispered.

"That's better. Now. You're going to marry me."

"I have a choice? No! Don't——"

"You're going to marry me?"

"Yes."

"You can't help yourself because you love me?"

"Yes."

"And if I want to dig a coal mine in front of this house you'll smile sweetly and applaud?"

A little silence. Not very much of one. He was too close, the pattern had been set, the truth had been paraded up in front of the whole world, and besides he smelled so magnificently male, and, she told herself, I wouldn't mind at all finding out what the next act is! He jogged her gently. "Yes," she said hurriedly. "Yes!"

"I guess that's enough for the first lesson," he said. "Why are you looking so disappointed?"

Not me, she told herself firmly. You don't get a statement out of me on that score. I wasn't born yesterday. I know all about male-female relationships. Well, I know *some* things about relationships. Lift up the banner of women's rights!

"Put me down," she insisted, and was totally surprised when he did just that. "When I get married I don't expect to become a house slave," she said. "I believe in women's rights, and I mean to have some! Women are the equal of man any time!"

"I *knew* there'd be trouble," he said, shaking his head dolefully. "In the old Croatian system I'd end up beating you for saying things like that."

"Well you'd better not try," she snapped. "You're too old a Croatian to get away with it. I'm a big girl!"

"Indeed you are," he said, chuckling. "And I wouldn't know what to do with a subservient woman. No, lady, a marriage is shared. But remember this, in marriage men and women are complementary to each other, not identical. You get to run the house, balance the budget, order the children around——"

"What house?"

"*This* house. I've decided not to open a coal mine on the front lawn. The kids might fall in. We're going to live here. You and I and Nora and John Junior and Harry and Katie..."

He was too close to miss. She kissed the end of his nose, and got into the spirit of things. "But after our son Vanya is born," she said, "we're going to buy a television, or maybe go to the movies more often."

"I knew you'd get the hang of it!" He laughed as he threw her up in the air again—and missed catching her!

"Oh, Lord!" she gasped. "We're not even married yet, and you've broken my back!"

"Yeah, well," he sighed. "The spirit was willing—you weigh an awful lot, love." He knelt down beside her, all commiseration, running his hands up and down her body from ankle to nose—and back again. And again.

"I don't feel anything broken," he muttered as he worked his way up from her hip and stopped halfway. "How do you get this thing off?"

"There's a zipper in the back," she teased. He fumbled for another moment or two, and then muttered something that sounded like "Oh, hell!".

So very suddenly that Kate could not understand the change, she was panting for breath, perspiring like mad, trembling in all her joints, wishing . . . !

He seemed to snatch at her frantically, as if unable to wait another moment. Back in his arms again, still shuddering, she ducked her head into his shoulder as he strode up the stairs, stomped down the hall, and kicked the door of her bedroom open. Despite her own desperation, her own tension, Kate spared one loving look at the man—her man. He was puffing under her weight, and the steepness of the stairs, but he was not about to quit—until he came to the side of her big four-poster bed, where his breath ran out, making a whistling noise the way an emptying teakettle might do, and he dropped her right in the middle of the bed.

The bed was old but well-sprung. Kate felt herself bounce a time or two, and could not keep from laughing. Her skirt had gone awry, and he had managed to find the zip on her blouse. He stood at the side of the bed, hands on hips, and glared at her as he rocked back and forth on the soles of his feet.

"Woman," he said fiercely, "don't you ever laugh at your husband."

"I'll remember that, just in case we might get married," she giggled.

He had rocked too far. His bulk toppled over on her. He managed to get his hands out just enough so that he didn't squash her, but he did effectively pin her down.

"Just in case? Damn. What you need is a good lesson! I'm going to——"

"I wish you would," she giggled.

"What's going on here?" A squeaky little voice from the doorway. Nora, standing just inside the room, hands on hips, her face red with anger. "Don't you dare hurt Kate. I need her!" A moment of absolute silence, and then a brilliant smile flashed across the little face.

"Oh! I know what you're doing. You're making a baby!"

"Where in the world did you learn something like that?" her father spluttered.

"I know lots of things," Nora replied. "Susie Sandson's in the sixth grade—for the second time—and she told me that when her mother and father fight on the bed that's what they're doing. Isn't that wonderful?" With which she sparkled a kiss at each of them, and turned and walked out of the room, carefully closing the door behind her.

Kate rolled over on her side to face him. "My goodness," Kate murmured as her fingers began to struggle with the buttons on his shirt. "What a clever child you have."

"*We* have," he grumbled. "But if she gets on the telephone to tell her grandmother my name will be mud."

"She might do that?" Kate's face was as red as her rambling roses. Red but determined.

"She might just do that," Jack Lee said. "Well, as long as I've already got that name, Mrs. Mud, why don't we——?"

"I thought you'd never ask," Kate moaned. "Hurry up! We have direct-distance dialing in this county!"

HARLEQUIN PRESENTS®

BARBARY WHARF

**Home to the *Sentinel*
Home to passion, heartache and love**

The **BARBARY WHARF** six-book saga continues with Book
Five, **A SWEET ADDICTION**. Guy Faulkner and Sophie Watson
have both been abandoned by the people they love, but is that
reason enough to find themselves in each other's arms? It isn't
for Sophie. And it isn't the kind of solace Gina Tyrrell wants
from Nick Caspian, either—despite the fact that she's becoming
increasingly confused about her feelings for the tall, handsome
man. But love them or leave them, these men just won't go away!

**A SWEET ADDICTION (Harlequin Presents #1530)
available in February.**